I0788400

Goose Princess

GOOSE PRINCESS

A Goose Girl & Wild Swans Retelling
Beyond the Tales Book Four

TRICIA MINGERINK

Sword & Cross Publishing

The Seven Kingdoms
of Tallahatchia
Castle Fonthaven
Pohatomie River
Pohatomie
Buckhannock
Buckhannock River
Monongadotte
Monongadotte River
Castle Firlin
Rand Clan Home
Kanawhee
Chattakee
Gaulee River
Nanooga
Neskahana
Cheyandoah Trace
Onohio River
Castle Eyota
Clearwater Creek
Castle Deeling
Neskahana River
Kanawhee River
Kikataw
Grassy Lick Creek
Fishrock Cove
Fort Last Chance
Guyangahela
Tuckawassee
Aunt Frennie's Cabin
Nanahootchie Creek
Guyangahela River
Castle Greenbrier
Tuckawassee River

CHAPTER 1

ALEXANDER

igh King Alexander of Tallahatchia dipped his paddle into the still waters of the Kanawhee River. The prow of his canoe parted the shrouding morning mist lying thick over the river and clinging to the surrounding mountains. The faintest blush of pink painted the horizon and highlighted the edges of the summer leaves.

For a moment, he rested his paddle across his knees and let his canoe drift with the current. He drew in a deep breath of the misty air tinged with the muddy wet of the river and crisp green of the trees crowding the banks.

Closing his eyes, he soaked in the sounds of the awakening mountains, from the birds chorusing their praise for the day the Highest King had given to the ripples of the river shushing against the sides of his birchbark canoe.

Peace. He'd been fighting so hard for it in the three years since he'd woken from his cursed sleep. Peace for Tallahatchia...and for himself.

It would seem he had succeeded in the first. With

Queen Tamya on the throne of Tuckawassee, that kingdom was once again loyal to him as the High King.

Only King Cassius of Pohatomie remained a danger, and he had lain low in the past two years, ever since he'd married Princess Uma of Tuckawassee.

That left peace for himself. Alex drew in another deep breath. On mornings like this, such a thing didn't seem so far out of reach either.

From upriver, the faint sounds of splashing, the thump of wood on wood, the tromp of feet, and men's voices singing in rhythm floated through the fog. One of the keelboats, making its way to Eyota.

Alex shook himself and dipped his paddle into the water once again, sending his canoe gliding downriver. His guards fell into place around him, as protective as a gaggle of geese around a gosling.

While he missed Daemyn and Rosanna, he rather liked the mornings when they weren't here. He enjoyed a leisurely morning paddle instead of shooting the rapids on the Gaulee.

A pang shot through him. Daemyn and Rosanna had been traveling in northern Buckhannock this spring, visiting his family and exploring more of Buckhannock.

But it had been over a week since they'd last sent a message, something that was unusual for them. Thanks to Daemyn's network of family scattered throughout Tallahatchia, Daemyn usually kept Alex apprised of their whereabouts.

Worse, they had been supposed to arrive at Castle Firlin, the stronghold of Buckhannock, a few days ago. Alex hadn't been told all the details, but he'd gathered there was some family matter Daemyn needed to attend to at Castle Firlin in the coming days.

That just made his and Rosanna's disappearance all the more suspicious. Daemyn was nothing if not loyal to his family. He would move the mountains of Tallahatchia before he missed an important event in their lives.

It could be nothing. Perhaps Daemyn and Rosanna would send a message that very day with some highly entertaining tale of how they'd been delayed.

Or they were in trouble.

As the sounds of the keelboat grew louder, Alex's guards closed ranks. Captain Taum directed Alex to steer his canoe closer to the center of the river.

Alex glanced over his shoulder as the keelboat turned the corner, breaking through the mist. Rows of men with long poles marched on either side of the boat next to the raised center, which covered the cargo. A few passengers perched on the raised cargo hold.

Alex smiled, lifting a hand to wave at the captain at the tiller. While Alex had slept, river travel had become nearly nonexistent. Now that the war was over and the kingdoms could turn their warriors to keeping the rivers safe from pirates, the trade along the rivers was booming again. The keelboats had come back, plying these waters as they had a hundred years ago.

Another piece of Tallahatchia put back together.

The keelboat's captain lifted a hand from the tiller to wave back. A few of the passengers also waved. Or bowed, if they realized that was their High King drifting in his canoe.

Once the keelboat passed, Alex steered his canoe into the boat's wake, letting the keelboat get farther downriver before he paddled in earnest.

As he and his guards drew closer to Eyota, the river grew more crowded with keelboats, large dugout canoes carrying trade goods, and smaller birchbark canoes like Alex's.

High on the mountain above, the spires of Castle Eyota cast long shadows onto the cliff face. The red sandstone walls gleamed in the morning sunlight, turning the castle even more pink.

They could have turned into the palace dock below the castle, but they kept going, instead pulling the canoes alongside one of the docks jutting into the river before Eyota.

Alex climbed from his canoe as a dock worker hurried to take the canoe from him.

"I'll take your canoe, Your Majesty." The worker gripped the prow, giving Alex an affable grin.

"Thank you." Alex nodded to the lad before he strode up the dock, his guards falling into place around him.

The bustle of Eyota's streets parted around Alex, though people stepped aside mostly with smiles and bows rather than annoyed looks. He had to duck around the huge, horned headdresses worn by those from Monongadotte, even as he brushed against the brightly garbed traders from Guyangahela. Eyota was filled with a myriad of skin colors, from the dark-skinned Tuckawassee to the pale Pohatomie.

Most of the shops and homes in Eyota were new, having been rebuilt out of the decay of the past hundred years. Now—as it had decades before—goods from all over Tallahatchia filled the shops and the market stalls. Beads and pottery from Neskahana. Furs and dried meats from Monongadotte. Fine cloth from Guyangahela and jewels from Tuckawassee. One vendor displayed knives forged in Buckhannock while booth upon booth was filled with the produce grown in the fertile fields of Pohatomie.

Tallahatchia was rising from the ashes of the hundred years of war.

Yet in many ways, this was better than Tallahatchia had been before. A hundred years ago, Tallahatchia had been wallowing in indolence and laxity when it came to following the Highest King. Now, Tallahatchia had gone through war. The kingdoms had been refined. The people had learned a new dependence on the Highest King.

As had Alex.

To the north side of Eyota, a stockade of thick logs penned in various pack animals, from shaggy buffalo to the occasional elk, as they grazed on the thick grass.

Alex halted next to a blonde-haired woman bouncing a baby on her hip and a young man holding out a carrot to one of the elk in the paddock.

"Your Majesty." The sandy-haired man bowed. His wife curtsied as much as she could while holding the baby.

"Terrence. Elara." Alex gestured for them to rise. No need for the two of them to stand on ceremony. Not after what the three of them had been through in Pohatomie a couple of years ago. "Welcome to Eyota. Are these the latest animals you've trained?"

"Yes." Terrence reached through the fence and rubbed the elk's nose as it crunched, slobbering and open-mouthed, on the carrot. "Most of these are already spoken for. Word of our trained animals has spread through Tallahatchia. I believe we have you to thank for that, Your Majesty."

"If word has spread, it's due to your skill." Alex reached through the fence and tentatively stroked the elk's fur as well. He had purchased a few of their trained buffalo to help with rebuilding efforts in Eyota. If the buffalo's training had gotten attention and sent business Terrence and Elara's way, then so much the better.

After glancing around, Terrence lowered his voice. "While we're here, we wanted to bring you news from Pohatomie."

Alex stiffened, also flicking a glance around to ensure they wouldn't be overheard.

His guards hung back, their presence preventing anyone else from approaching Alex and the others near the fence.

Alex forced his posture to relax in case anyone was watching. "I thought King Cassius has been rather quiet lately. I was hoping that his marriage had mellowed him."

Elara grimaced, still rocking her baby on her hip. "I highly doubt it. From what my sources have observed, poor Queen Uma hasn't been too happy. She and King Cassius are about as frosty as a midwinter night."

Against her sister's wishes, Princess Uma of Tuckawassee married King Cassius nearly two years ago now, shortly after their oldest sister was killed. While Alex had been hoping the marriage would bring King Cassius into line, it had been a faint hope.

Alex continued petting the elk as if this was no more than a casual conversation between friends. "I'm sorry to hear that Queen Uma has been so miserable."

"It has become worse lately. According to Monica and Beatrice, Queen Uma has been nearly silent at court functions, if she attends at all." Elara shook her head, her mouth pressed into a tight line. "Worse yet, more and more Tuckawassee warriors have been seen hanging around Castle Fonthaven. Pretty much anyone from Tuckawassee who isn't happy with Queen Tamya has been making their way to Pohatomie."

"A group of them recently disappeared into the forest and haven't been seen since." Terrence scratched the elk between his antlers. "Stefan Vinzen reached out to us when he heard we were heading here. He said to let you know that he reckons King Cassius has been planning something, though he doesn't know what it is. He's going to keep his ear to the ground."

Stefan Vinzen was Castle Fonthaven's seneschal...and one of Daemyn's many relatives. If he thought King Cassius was plotting something, then the situation wasn't good.

"Thank you for passing the information along." Alex gave the elk one last pat before he turned away from the fence.

That gnawing worry in his stomach grew worse. It wasn't that far from Pohatomie to northern Buckhannock.

What if Daemyn and Rosanna had been prevented from returning?

Perhaps it wasn't that serious. Maybe they were merely investigating the trouble on their own.

Alex would present the problem to the King's Council —the group of representatives from each kingdom who provided advice to the high king.

Then again, no matter what the King's Council said, Alex's mind was already made up. He needed to find Daemyn and Rosanna. If King Cassius was plotting something, Alex needed Daemyn's advice more than ever.

More than that, Daemyn was Alex's friend—his brother—in a way no one else was. He'd rallied his entire extended family to help Alex multiple times. The least Alex could do was show up when Daemyn and Rosanna needed him in return.

Chapter 2

Keziah

Princess Keziah of Buckhannock perched on the edge of her seat at the dinner table as she plotted how to ask for the potatoes.

Such a simple request...for anyone else besides her.

All royalty and nobility in Tallahatchia were given a gift and a curse on their eighth day. For some, like her brothers, the curse didn't hit right away. But for Kezzie, she'd lived with her curse her entire life, except for those first seven days of life. Not that she could even remember those first, glorious seven days. Such a waste.

Kezzie's curse was that she couldn't communicate with people. No talking. No gestures. Not even facial expressions with too much intent to communicate.

Thus her problem with the potatoes. She sat near the end of the long, oak table that filled the castle's dining room. Her two younger brothers, Josiah and Ezra, had the seats to her left and across from her. Her two older brothers Zephaniah and Zebediah—yes, her parents greatly regretted the choice of names that were so similar for the twins—had the seats next to them. Her parents sat at the far end with her grandfather, King Omri of Buckhannock, at the head of the table.

That elusive bowl of mashed potatoes rested near her father's plate. Far, far down the table.

"The scouts reported another sighting of Tuckawassee and Pohatomie warriors in Buckhannock." Father stabbed his venison steak with his fork. "We are supposedly at peace. They shouldn't be sending warriors within our borders."

"King Cassius has never appreciated peace unless it benefits him." Grandfather stirred butter into his mashed potatoes, the deep lines in his face making him appear even more weary. At over eighty years old, Grandfather had witnessed many of the years of unrest when Tallahatchia had been without a high king.

Kezzie fiddled with her fork, taking a moment to plan out her words before she spoke to the utensil.

Yes, to the fork. Not to her brothers. Not to her family. But to the fork and only the fork. "You know, Fork, I really would appreciate it if my brothers passed the potatoes."

This was the work-around she'd figured out years ago. While she couldn't communicate with people, she could talk to objects and animals. It made her sound a touch crazy at times, but at least she could get her point across, as long as she mentally directed her words to the object or animal. If she tried to use it merely as a stand-in but really meant to talk with a person, the words would stick in the back of her throat.

But she couldn't address people to grab their attention. She couldn't even poke Josiah with her fork—satisfying as that would have been—because that would communicate too much.

Her brothers, leaning forward and turned away from her as they conversed with her parents and grandfather, didn't even seem to notice.

Kezzie suppressed a sigh. Normally her family was more aware of listening for her version of communication. But not tonight. Not with what was about to happen at midnight.

"It's especially concerning that Uncle Daemyn hasn't arrived." Zeph, the oldest of the twins and the crown prince, scooped another helping of mashed potatoes onto his plate. Because he, of course, had no trouble getting the potatoes passed to him.

"He promised he would be here." Ezra, the youngest of all her brothers, poked at his venison rather than eating it. Of all her brothers, he seemed the most lacking in appetite tonight. Understandable, considering it was his birthday—at midnight, to be precise—that would set off the curse on all four of her brothers.

The Fallen Fae dispensing curses on her brothers had been particularly uncreative, cursing all four brothers that they would turn into geese at midnight on the morning of their youngest brother's eighteenth birthday. Kezzie's parents had done their best to keep having boys to push off the curse as long as possible.

Why the Fallen Fae hadn't given Kezzie—the one girl sandwiched in the middle—the same curse, no one knew. Instead, the Fallen Fae had made up for the lack of creativity in the curses on Kezzie's brothers with a rather unique curse for Kezzie.

"It's Uncle Daemyn. He wouldn't miss our curse." Josiah sawed at his venison steak as if it were an enemy. His jaw worked, the muscle knotting beneath his dusky brown skin. He'd been the brother sent along with Uncle Daemyn on that trip into Pohatomie a few years ago. "Something must have happened to him and Rosanna."

Kezzie gulped and stared down at her plate, empty of everything but the juices from her finished steak.

Whatever had happened, it must have been rather serious. Uncle Daemyn wouldn't break a promise like this without a good reason.

He'd been there for all of them through the ups and downs. Thanks to a pledge he had made a hundred years ago, he had lived un-aging and more-or-less undying for a hundred years. All his siblings, including Kezzie's great-something grandfather Luke, had promised that they and their descendants would aid him.

It had created bonds within their family so strong that no amount of time or curses could break.

"We can't just sit here." Ezra flexed his fingers on his knife. "If Uncle Daemyn is in trouble, we need to help."

"We've already done everything we can." Zeb, the younger of the two twins, took the bowl of potatoes from Zeph. "And there isn't much we can do with our curse about to strike."

"I'm sure Zeke and Asa will find them." Josiah spoke around a bite of venison. "You'll see."

Kezzie couldn't even nod along in response, even if she agreed. Zeke—short for Ezekiel, as if they needed any more names starting with Z in this family—and Asa were brothers, coming from the branch of the Rand Clan that still lived on the ancestral mountain in western Buckhannock. If anyone could help Uncle Daemyn and Rosanna, they could.

Isi, Zeke's wife, was currently pregnant—hugely pregnant. As much as she had wanted to go after Rosanna, she'd been forced to stay behind here at Castle Firlin.

"My main concern is the curse." Mother joined the conversation for the first time. Soft-spoken as she was, she preferred to let her family do all the talking while she observed, until she had something to say.

Everyone quieted, turning to her. It would have been the perfect time to ask for the potatoes, but Kezzie wasn't going to interrupt her mother for something as paltry as potatoes.

"We have done our best to keep the nature of the curse quiet, but I fear King Cassius will have found a way to discover it." Mother's brow furrowed as she swept a glance over Zeph, Zeb, Josiah, and Ezra before she focused on Grandfather. "It could be the reason King Cassius is moving now. He couldn't strike us while we were strong, but we will be at our weakest once the curse strikes. If our sons were to be killed as men, it would be murder. But if four geese were to turn up dead, it could be passed off as an accident."

Now that put a pall on the whole table. Kezzie's steak churned in her stomach. She wasn't so hungry for the potatoes now.

With all four of her brothers soon to be geese and her unable to communicate with people and thus incapable of stepping into her true role as princess, her parents would be left essentially without an heir until one or more of their curses were broken.

This would be King Cassius's chance to cut off the line of Rand kings of Buckhannock. Such a thing would not only weaken Buckhannock, but also the whole Rand Clan. In the end, it would weaken High King Alexander's hold over Tallahatchia.

"It was one thing when Uncle Daemyn was going to be here." Mother sat straight in her chair, the upper part of her black hair in elaborate braids while the lower part remained straight down her back. "But the situation has changed now that Uncle Daemyn is missing. We must assume our sons will be in danger the moment they become geese."

"King Cassius can't touch them here in the castle." Father reached across the table to hold Mother's hand.

"Can't he?" Mother squeezed Father's fingers, her knuckles whitening. "The castle might be fortified, but he will also know right where they are. Even if King Cassius doesn't know about the curse now, he will once word spreads that four geese are being treated like princes at Castle Firlin."

Despite what must be a tight grip, Father didn't flinch or pull his hand free. He rubbed his thumb over the back of Mother's hand. "They will be well guarded."

"And we'll be geese." Zeb shrugged shoulders that were the broadest of her four brothers'. "We won't be helpless. You know how vicious geese can be."

Kezzie held up her fork again. "Fork, don't you think it would be funny if my brothers hid among the castle's flock of geese? They'd have to eat grass and bugs and pretend to be real geese."

This time her family actually heard her. Across the table, Ezra scowled. "I'm not eating bugs."

Josiah elbowed her. "You'd get a good laugh out of that, wouldn't you?"

"Fork, you'd make a great bug catcher. I could catch loads of bugs and feed them to my goose brothers." Kezzie inspected the tines of the fork.

Josiah rolled his eyes, and Ezra's scowl deepened.

Zeph rubbed his chin, eyeing her. "It isn't such a bad

idea. I doubt King Cassius's men could find four more geese among the castle's flock."

"Unless he has a man already inside the castle." Mother gripped Father's hand with both of hers.

"Even then, most people don't pay much attention to the castle's geese, except for the cook and the goose girl." Zeph crossed his arms. "Do you know how many geese are in the castle's flock? I certainly don't."

"Sixteen," Mother replied without missing a beat.

Kezzie closed her mouth. She, too, could have told them how many geese there were in the flock. She had long ago made pets of them. At least, all the geese that were kept for eggs and future population. She tried not to get too close to the ones that were slated to land on the table at once point.

But Mother had spoken up before Kezzie had the chance to formulate a way to speak.

"All right, Mother. You know. But you're the lady of the castle. It's your job to know that stuff. A Pohatomie spy will be more concerned with counting guards than counting geese." Zeph shoved his empty plate out of the way so he could better rest his elbows on the table as he leaned forward.

"It's a good idea." Zeb nodded, his mouth quirking. "Though I agree with Ezra. I won't be eating any bugs."

"I don't know. If bugs taste like steak to a goose, perhaps it won't be so bad." Josiah eyed the last bite of his steak. "It isn't like we'll be eating steak once we're geese."

"No steak." Ezra sighed down at his empty plate.

"But we'll be able to fly. That will be something." Josiah grinned. "I've been looking forward to that."

Mother shot Josiah a quelling look, as if she didn't

appreciate that Josiah would find anything fun about the coming curse.

At the head of the table, Grandfather cleared his throat. "Perhaps we should take Kezzie's idea a step farther. Once the curse strikes, Zeph, Zeb, Josiah, and Ezra can fly to the Rand Clan in the mountains. They'll be hidden there. We can pretend four of the castle's geese are the princes, stationing extra guards around them. If King Cassius tries to move against us, all he will do is kill four geese, and any spies he has at the castle will have tipped their hand."

Father nodded, though grooves still bracketed his deep frown. "Wouldn't the trip to the mountains place them in more danger? Even if King Cassius doesn't realize they are traveling, they would be at the mercy of hunters. Nor would they be able to speak to tell the family who they are."

A problem. But one Kezzie could solve.

"Oh, a trip! I'd have to take you along, Fork." Kezzie held the fork in both hands as she addressed it. "Don't worry about getting lost. I know the way to the Rand Clan's home in the mountains very well. And we won't be in any danger. Who would pay attention to a simple goose girl traveling through the mountains with her flock of geese?"

Her whole family turned to her again, though she only saw the looks they were sending her out of the corner of her eye as she didn't dare break her focus on the fork and lose the ability to respond.

"It...might work." Grandfather nodded, stroking his chin. "Kezzie has spent most of her life secluded here in the castle or living in the mountains with the Rand Clan.

While any spies here might know her, the rest of King Cassius's warriors won't."

"It would still be dangerous." Father still held Mother's hands, even as his jaw worked. "If we could send a squad of guards along, I'd feel better, but that would give away the ruse."

"If only Zeke or Asa had remained here." Mother's gaze rested on Kezzie, though Kezzie didn't turn to meet her eyes.

"What are we, helpless goldfinches?" Josiah gestured to himself. "We'll be geese, Mother. *Geese*. With sharp beaks and everything."

Even in the corner of her eye, Kezzie could make out the glint to Josiah's gaze and smile. He was planning something...something that he thought going into the hills would get him.

Perhaps more freedom to fly? Here at the castle, her brothers would be so tightly guarded that they wouldn't be allowed to stretch their new wings.

"Perhaps you're right, Fork. You aren't enough of a weapon." Kezzie held the fork in one hand and patted the long knife belted at her hip. "I'll take Conrad and Nettle. I'm quite skilled with Nettle, I'll have you know."

Those were the names she'd given to her knife and her bow. It was easier to talk to objects in her possession if she named them.

"See? Kezzie's right. She's quite good with her bow." Josiah waved to her. "We'll be protection for Kezzie, and she'll be protection for us. It's perfect."

"All right, but if we're going to do this, we'll send a message to the family tonight to let them know to watch for Kezzie and the boys." Mother released Father's hand, some of her unflinching posture returning. "I'll ask Leah if she's willing to impersonate Kezzie. She looks similar enough that she might be able to fool a Pohatomie spy from a distance."

Kezzie's chest seized. Leah was Kezzie's maid and guard. She was also a cousin. Kind of. She was descended from the same great-something Grandpa Luke. In a normal family, she and Kezzie wouldn't even be closely related enough to consider each other family.

But they were Rands. And Rands were family, no matter how tenuous the connection.

Leah would do whatever it took to protect Kezzie, even impersonate her and take on the risk of being attacked. That was what Rands did for each other.

"Then it's settled." Father swept a glance around the table. "You'll all leave first thing in the morning before word spreads and King Cassius has time to put any of his plans into action."

The others around the table nodded. A solemn silence descended on the room.

If she still wanted the potatoes, now was her chance. Kezzie held up her fork again. "In that case, Fork, I will need to keep my strength up. Could you please fetch the potatoes?"

She gave the fork a light toss. It landed with a clatter near the bowl of potatoes by Zeb's plate.

Zeb picked up the bowl and the fork. "Sorry, Kezzie. There isn't much left."

The bowl and fork were passed down the table before Josiah set both of them in front of her.

She picked up the bowl and suppressed a sigh. Only a crusting of mashed potatoes remained around the sides of the bowl along with a mouthful or two resting at the bottom.

Taking her spoon, she scraped off the last of the pota-toes and popped the rather sad, cold bite into her mouth. She shouldn't begrudge her brothers the potatoes. After tonight, they would be geese and wouldn't be eating meals like mashed potatoes and steak for who knew how long.

Grandfather pushed to his feet, his wizened features stern. "I have one last thing to say. It's natural to fear a curse. They are terrible things, as they are meant to be, for they are symbols of the greater curse we all carry in our hearts. But we are sons and daughters of the Lord of All Fae and Men. He has promised a cursebreaker, both for the symbolic curses and the true curse. His promises are sure, more sure than the foundations of the mountains. I urge all of you to face this curse with unflinching courage and the unwavering hope that it will be broken in his timing."

For the first time during that supper, Ezra sat straight, the despondency sloughing off him. Josiah nodded with a grave solemnity, though he couldn't entirely bury his grin. Zeb remained as he was with his arms crossed, though something about the set of his shoulders and the tightness in his muscles relaxed. Zeph glanced between each of them, still prepared to be the leader once he was a goose.

Kezzie swallowed, fighting back the words that wanted to burst from her, if she could have spoken directly back to her grandfather.

It was so easy for him to say that. But he'd only been under his own curse for a few months before his was broken. Even her brothers at least had normal childhoods.

But she'd been living with her curse for twenty-three years. Twenty-three years of never having a normal conver-sation. Of struggling to make friends outside of the family. Of growing up seeing people's laughter at the way she talked to objects and animals. Twenty-three years with no end in sight and no idea when—or if—her cursebreaker would come.

Perhaps it made her weak. Or a bad follower of the Highest King. But sometimes she just wanted to scream at him.

But it wouldn't do any good. Even if she traveled all the way to the halls of the threshold of Beyond—as it was said Uncle Daemyn and High King Alexander had done over a hundred years ago—she likely wouldn't even be able to speak to the Highest King, thanks to her curse.

Zeph pushed his chair back and stood. "In that case, I don't want to spend my last few hours as a human moping around. Let's call for a fiddle and have a good ol' fashioned hoedown until midnight."

Josiah let out a holler and hopped to his feet. Ezra wasn't far behind him.

Kezzie joined the rush from the dining room to the Great Hall. Within a few minutes, a servant hurried in, carrying a fiddle. As he sawed out a rousing tune, Kezzie's family whirled into a jig. Without Zeke or Asa to cut a mountain jig, it wasn't quite as impressive, but Kezzie threw herself into the dance anyway.

For a few hours, the night disappeared into dancing and music, laughter and smiles.

But as midnight approached, the steps grew slower, the glances at the clock by the door more frequent.

Eventually, Father called a halt and dismissed the fiddler. The eight of them gathered in the center of the room, a tense silence replacing the music and joy of a moment before.

"Well, this is it." Zeb rested an arm on Ezra's shoulder.

Ezra hunched as he stared at the clock. "Maybe nothing will happen."

It was a faint hope. Everyone knew one couldn't escape a curse. Many people had tried over the years. Even High King Alexander had tried to avoid his hundred years of sleep. But none of them, not even the high king, had succeeded. There was no escaping. Just accepting.

Zeph clapped Ezra on his other shoulder. "So we'll turn into geese. We'll be fine. All curses will be broken, even ours. We have nothing to fear."

Ezra flicked a gaze to Kezzie, as if he was thinking the same thing she was. All curses were promised to be broken, but some took an awfully long time to break. High King Alexander had to wait a hundred years before his was broken. She'd already been waiting twenty-three years. How long would her brothers have to wait?

But after a moment, Ezra looked away from Kezzie and pasted on a grin once again. "Thanks, everyone. Still not looking forward to getting feathers. But at least we'll all be together, feathers or no."

"And we'll be able to fly." Josiah stepped in and slapped Ezra on the back.

As the second hand of the clock ticked away until midnight, Father and Mother embraced each of Kezzie's brothers, and if Mother's cheeks were wet, no one mentioned it.

Kezzie would have hugged her brothers too, but her curse wouldn't let her communicate that much. Even if one of them initiated a hug, she still wouldn't be able to hug back.

Josiah pulled her into the family huddle. They stood like that for long moments as if unwilling to let each other go, waiting for the stroke of midnight to tear them apart.

Then it came. The clock began the notes marking out the midnight hour. It struck once. Twice.

Around Kezzie, her brothers began to change. Shrink. Turn soft and feathery beneath her hands.

By the time the clock struck twelve, Kezzie was surrounded by four brown geese with black necks and white markings on their faces.

One of the geese gave a honk, flapping his wings. Another twisted his long black neck around to inspect himself.

A third goose tucked close to Kezzie, as if begging for a hug.

She bent and rested a hand on his back. "Ezra?" Then realizing what she had just done, she clapped a hand over her mouth.

Father stared from her to the goose, then back. Then a smile slowly crossed his face. "They're stuck in animal form right now. That must be enough to get around your curse, Kezzie."

For the first time in her life, she could speak to her brothers.

As the sunrise stained the clouds above the castle walls, Kezzie ran her fingers over her beloved canoe Falada, the birchbark sides painted with bright designs. "Time for another adventure, Falada."

Uncle Daemyn, Zeph, and Zeb made this canoe for her when she was barely big enough to paddle it. She'd paddled many miles up and down the Buckhannock River in it, traveling between Castle Firlin and the sanctuary of the peaceful Rand ancestral home in the mountains. Whenever she needed to cry over a mean comment or vent her frustration at her curse, she'd take

Falada out onto the river and pour her words out to the canoe.

Sure, the canoe couldn't speak back. It was just an object. But it was far more than just a canoe to her.

Behind her, Mother and Father knelt as they said farewells to Kezzie's brothers, who were now four brown and black geese.

"Here's your pack, Your Highness." Leah set a large travel pack by Kezzie's feet. Her black hair lay long over her shoulders, her oval face bearing some resemblance to the shape of Kezzie's.

Kezzie took the pack, securing it in the center of the canoe and placing her oilskin-wrapped bow and arrows on top. She kept her gaze squarely on Falada's peaked prow. "Falada, I wish I could tell you how grateful I am for what Leah is doing for us. She's risking so..."

Kezzie's words cut off in her throat. She'd gotten too personal, speaking too much toward Leah and not enough toward Falada.

"It's my honor, Your Highness." Leah knelt, then gently gave Kezzie a hug. "We're Rands. We look out for each other. I can't join in the search for Uncle Daemyn, but I can do this. Now focus on keeping your brothers safe. We'll have things well in hand here."

Kezzie couldn't even nod, much less reply with a thank you. Instead, she turned to Falada again. "What do you think, Falada? I think my dresses will look rather lovely on Leah. She'll pull this off."

Leah smiled at that, gesturing to Kezzie. "I'd say my clothes will look good on you, but you already have your own set of basic buckskins for travel."

Kezzie smoothed her hand over her fringed pants, blue cotton shirt, and fringed jacket. In this get-up, she looked like any one of the mountain girls traveling the Buckhannock River. If needed, Kezzie could even speak with a decent mountain accent.

After another moment, Leah straightened, then gave a small curtsy as Mother approached.

Mother smiled at Leah, shaking her head. "You'll have to break that habit."

"Yes, Your...Yes." Leah seemed to lock her knees, as if resisting another curtsy. She didn't say "Mother." Perhaps calling the queen by that particular title was too strange, even while pretending to be Kezzie.

Kezzie stood, and Mother pulled her in for a hug. "Stay safe and stay alert. I know you know the way, but the trip will still be dangerous."

Kezzie glanced over her shoulder, focusing on her canoe. "Falada, we'll be just fine. You have gotten me there safely lots of times. I reckon you'll do it again."

Mother gave her yet another hug before Father joined them, wrapping an arm around Kezzie's shoulders. "I'm counting on you to look after your brothers. I know half of them are older than you and usually do the looking after. But they're geese right now. You have a good head on your shoulders. I reckon you'll get them through this."

Kezzie couldn't nod or hug him back. But perhaps he understood, for he gave her one last pat on the back before pulling away.

With the sun rising, they couldn't linger. Kezzie and her brothers needed to be on their way before any people were out and about to see them leave.

Kezzie took in her parents' faces one last time. The green slope of the mountainside rose behind them with the gray stone walls of Castle Firlin rising at the top, silhouetted against the pink of the morning. How long would it be before it was safe to return home?

With a deep breath, Kezzie climbed into Falada's rear seat, took up her paddle, and shoved away from the bank.

Flapping and honking uproariously, the four geese trundled down the bank, as awkward and stumbling as goslings. One of them tripped and fell chest-first onto the ground, neck splayed out in front of him.

Only one of them managed to flap his way into the air. The other three splashed into the water, swimming alongside Kezzie for a few minutes.

"Flying isn't as easy as you thought it would be, Josiah?" Kezzie eyed the three geese in the water, reveling in the ability to talk directly to her brothers.

The one on the right gave her a honk and a sour look. That one must be Josiah. If she were to guess, Zeph was the goose in the air.

With something like a hop-skip-flap, one of the geese heaved himself out of the water, gained enough air beneath him to clear the side of the canoe, and plopped onto Falada's front seat.

"Let me guess. Ezra." Kezzie paused paddling long enough to poke the goose with her paddle.

He gave a honk, biting at the paddle with his beak. She took that as a *yes, and don't poke me.*

"All right. If you're going to be lazy, you can hitch a ride in the canoe." Kezzie dug her paddle into the river once again. She had to put her back and shoulders into it, going upriver as they were. "But you're going to have to figure out how to fly eventually. You can't sit in the canoe the whole way."

Ezra ruffled his feathers again, turning slightly on the bench seat to put his feathered tail toward her.

Kezzie couldn't help but laugh. Her brothers might be geese, but for the first time in her life, she could *talk* with them. Really talk.

Despite the danger, this trip might just be the best experience of her life.

ALEXANDER

After a week and a half of travel, Alex's muscles ached from the days of paddling his canoe. He'd hoped that the mornings on the Gaulee and Kanawhee had toughened up his muscles, but apparently sustained travel was still beyond his level of fitness.

At least his hands had some calluses built up. He'd only incurred a few mild blisters that didn't even burst before turning into additional calluses.

The Buckhannock River spread out before him, broad and fast-flowing, winding between the mountains. His guards filled the canoes around him, with Captain Taum leading the way.

This was the first time he'd traveled outside of Kanawhee without Daemyn at his side. The first time he'd traveled in a canoe all by himself. The first time he hadn't had his friends there to laugh with during the long hours of paddling.

While he'd tried to learn his guards' names and talk

with them, they were too focused on their duty as his guards to engage in much chitchat.

Alex sucked in a breath at the painful ache deep in his chest. Were Daemyn and Rosanna all right?

Hopefully, he would reach Castle Firlin and find Daemyn and Rosanna there, unable to send a message to Castle Eyota, for some perfectly innocent and inconsequential reason. Perhaps they'd even sent a message while Alex had been traveling.

Highly unlikely, but Alex could hope.

Alex and his guards swept around a bend in the river. Here, the mountains crowded closer, forming a faster section of river that rippled with whitewater as it whipped into the next bend. The water foamed against a large tree that had fallen across the bend, blocking most of the river.

Captain Taum held up a hand, letting his canoe drift. "That tree was cut down."

Alex dug his paddle in, slowing his canoe and fighting the current, as the rest of the guards turned their canoes to form a tighter knot around him.

Chop marks sliced into the tree's base, stark and fresh against the dark bark, instead of the root ball that should have been there if it had fallen over in a storm.

Perhaps a woodsman had cut it down, intending to float it down the river. By why leave such a large log unattended and abandoned?

Or it had been cut and left deliberately to block the river. Which could only mean one thing.

A trap.

"Your Majesty, we should seek the protection of the forest." Captain Taum scanned both banks in a swift glance, as if trying to assess which riverbank would hold safety and which sheltered waiting attackers. "Guards, head for—"

Arrows sliced from the forest on the far side of the river, splashing short of their canoes. If not for Captain Taum's sharp eyes and his orders halting them here, they would have been forced close to that bank by the log.

"Head for the north bank!" Captain Taum motioned to them, even as he turned his canoe to put himself between the far shore and Alex.

Heart beating harder, Alex dug his paddle in, aiming for the shore. Who was attacking them? Buckhannock had never been plagued by river pirates, as other kingdoms had been, thanks to Daemyn's family holding this kingdom together more effectively than the others.

Was it King Cassius's men? Former Tuckawassee warriors?

It didn't matter who they were. Right now, Alex needed to get into cover before any of his guards were hurt defending him.

No sooner did he pull into the shelter of the bank than the guards yanked him from his canoe, hustled him up the bank, and shoved him into cover at the base of a large oak tree. He could barely see what was going on past the backs of his guards.

Captain Taum splashed from the river, abandoning his canoe. "Get the high king—"

An arrow slammed into Captain Taum's shoulder. The force spun him, knocking him to the ground.

A war cry rang from the forest, followed by the crashing of many people charging downhill.

Alex reached for his knife. The first ambush had merely been a ploy to send them straight into the arms of this second attack.

The nearest guard grabbed Alex's arm and hauled him to his feet. "Run, Your Majesty!"

"We'll hold them off!" The other guards formed a cordon between them and the attackers.

Alex stumbled as the lone guard dragged him in the opposite direction of the charging attackers. He didn't want to leave his guards to fight alone while he ran like a coward.

But his guards would give their lives for him. The least he could do was keep himself safe. Perhaps the attackers would retreat, once he had gotten away.

With one last glance at his guards, Alex gathered his feet beneath him and dashed into the forest. He rested a hand on the long knife at his waist, but he didn't draw it yet. Running through the forest with a drawn knife sounded like a great way to accidentally stab himself.

His remaining guard kept pace with him, his hand also on his knife as his gaze darted about, searching for more attackers.

Alex scoured the forest as he raced along a hint of a game trail that followed the meandering riverbank. Should he look for a place to hide? Or keep running?

If he stuck to the river, he could reach Castle Firlin in several days on foot. That would mean giving up his guards for lost, since it would be a week or so before help would arrive from the castle.

He and his guard dashed around a stand of trees growing thick beside boulders that had long ago tumbled from the mountainside. If he was going to hide, this would be—

A hand grabbed him, yanking his arm behind his back. The edge of a knife pressed cold and sharp beneath his throat.

His heart pounding, his mind whirling, Alex stilled. Turning his head, he could just make out the blond hair and lighter skin of his captor. A warrior from Pohatomie.

Alex's guard froze, eyes wide, hand on his knife, though he didn't draw it. He wouldn't dare make a move that would risk Alex's life.

A blond-haired man wearing buckskins strode out of hiding from behind a tree, a thin smirk creasing his face. "High King Alexander. Thank you for running straight into my trap."

"King Cassius." Alex glared at the Pohatomie king. He should have known King Cassius would be behind all of this. Though, it was quite arrogant of the king to come himself.

Alex shifted his posture slightly. Could he draw his knife without either King Cassius or the warrior noticing?

"I knew once you lost contact with Daemyn Rand that you'd come to investigate." King Cassius sauntered closer, pulling a pristine white handkerchief from a pouch at his waist. "So predictable."

"What have you done with Daemyn? Where is he?" Alex yanked against the warrior holding him, turning his body as he did so. Still ostensibly fighting the warrior, Alex slipped his knife from its sheath.

Alex's guard hurried a step forward, his fingers closing on the hilt of his own knife.

"Not another step." The Pohatomie warrior tightened his grip, the edge of his knife slicing into Alex's skin. The warm, wet dribble of blood trickled down Alex's neck.

Alex's guard froze, jaw working. Alex met his gaze, then flicked his eyes toward King Cassius. The guard's brows furrowed, and Alex did it again. After a moment, the guard tilted his head in the slightest of nods as he eased a step back.

Hopefully he'd understood Alex's silent message. When Alex fought off the Pohatomie warrior, his guard needed to go for King Cassius.

"My warriors have been keeping him rather busy." King Cassius shook the handkerchief out. "Daemyn Rand won't be your concern much longer."

There was something about that handkerchief. It might be a shining white, but it sent cold prickles across Alex's skin, the kind of shivery feeling he recognized all too well.

That handkerchief was dangerous. More dangerous than the knife at Alex's throat.

Alex hid his hand and knife against his leg. "You won't get away with this, whatever this is. The rest of Tallahatchia is loyal to me. They won't take an attack on the high king lightly."

"They won't even know you've been attacked." King Cassius leaned forward and dabbed the handkerchief against the blood trickling from the shallow cut on Alex's neck. Three blots of blood stained the pristine white. "I acquired this token from the Fae. I had the idea for the request from that little stunt that servant girl pulled during your visit a few years ago. If this works as I was told, then no one will ever realize you have disappeared."

Alex tried not to tense as he subtly readied himself. "You don't know what you're messing with. That handkerchief must have been given to you by a Fallen Fae. A gift from them is only meant for deception and evil."

"Deception is exactly what I want, in this case." King Cassius folded the handkerchief into a neat square, then tucked it inside his shirt.

Instantly, something blurred about King Cassius. For a moment, it was like Alex was looking into a mirror. High King Alexander stood before him, dark brown hair tied back, an eagle feather dangling in the strands. A gold circlet graced his regal brow, and Alex's knees nearly buckled with the urge to bow before his high king.

A trickle of a breeze brushed against the back of Alex's neck like a cold dousing of river water. What was he thinking. *He* was the high king.

It wasn't real. This was a deception, just like those glass slippers a Fallen Fae had given Elara years ago. Just like the cursed dance in Tuckawassee.

Alex had seen more than his fair share of curses. And this was definitely a curse.

He blinked, and King Cassius was once again King Cassius.

Alex's guard stepped forward, bowing to King Cassius. "Your Majesty, what are your orders?"

King Cassius looked past Alex, focusing first on the warrior holding him, then on Alex's guard. "I see the handkerchief is working."

Alex gritted his teeth, readying himself. He was on his own.

King Cassius smirked at Alex, his posture dripping with triumphant arrogancy. "Now that I have your blood, I don't need you." He pointed a languid finger at Alex's chest. "Guards, that man is impersonating—"

Alex didn't wait for him to finish the order. He stabbed his knife into the Pohatomie warrior's thigh.

The warrior cried out, dropping his own knife and releasing Alex.

Alex yanked his blade out, dodged his own guard's thrusting knife, and lunged at King Cassius. The

Pohatomie king threw himself backwards, but Alex managed a swipe that sliced the king's arm.

King Cassius cried out and stumbled farther back, fumbling for his own knife.

The warrior behind Alex was straightening, reaching for his knife even as he pressed a hand to his wounded leg. Alex's guard, too, gathered himself for another attack.

Shoving past King Cassius, Alex sprinted into the forest, not looking back. His heart thundered in his ears, his blood pounding through his veins. He kept a tight hold on his knife, despite the danger of running with the drawn blade. There was no way he was losing his grip on his only weapon.

He raced through the forest as fast as he could, keeping the river in sight. The steep slope threatened to take his feet out from under him if he put his foot down wrong while the undergrowth and tree branches scraped at his arms and face.

No matter how hard his panting breaths came or how perilous his footing, he couldn't falter. If King Cassius wanted to pull this off, then he couldn't let Alex live.

Hopefully the injuries Alex had dealt King Cassius and his warrior were enough to slow them down.

Were his guards all right? Would Cassius kill them?

No, he wouldn't. Based on the way Alex's guard had reacted, the rest of the guards would be taken in by the curse as well. King Cassius's deception would be much more convincing if he had Alex's guards surrounding him.

Likely, King Cassius would give a signal, and his men would retreat into the forest as prearranged. King Cassius would saunter out of the forest with the one guard at his side as if nothing had happened.

What story would he tell them? That he'd run into

King Cassius in the forest and killed him? That before he died, King Cassius had confessed that Daemyn was dead, so they should just turn around and head back to Castle Eyota? For surely that would be King Cassius's destination, eager as he would be to take Alex's throne.

A shout and a crash came from the undergrowth somewhere behind Alex.

Alex nearly choked on his panting breath. Before King Cassius staged his return in Alex's place, he planned to ensure that Alex was well and truly dead.

Something on the river caught his eye. A canoe rounded a bend, coming from downstream. The young woman paddling the canoe was dressed in simple buckskin, her dark brown hair in a braid. A large pack took up the center of the canoe with a quiver of arrows and an unstrung bow resting on top. One goose perched on the prow of the canoe while a couple more swam next to the canoe.

Most likely a local goose girl, paddling along the river to one of the side creeks to find a new feeding spot for her geese.

He didn't want to endanger an innocent local girl, but right now, she was his one chance at surviving this.

Heart in his throat, his back tensing at having to break cover and expose himself to an arrow, Alex slid down the embankment and clambered onto a rock partway into the river.

He didn't dare shout to get her attention. Sound would carry. But he waved his arms, motioning her toward the bank.

Would she turn her canoe? She was a woman alone. The smart thing for her to do was keep paddling past him as quickly as she could.

If she did that, those chasing Alex would catch him and kill him before he'd have a chance to dive back into the cover of the forest.

Her gaze lifted to his, her deep brown eyes widening slightly. She didn't wave back, call out, or otherwise give any indication that she understood what he was trying to communicate.

But she turned her canoe toward him.

CHAPTER 4

KEZIAH

Kezzie turned her canoe toward the bank. What was High King Alexander doing here? Alone? Gripping a knife with a blade stained red?

In the prow of the canoe, Ezra swiveled his head, giving her a honk as he flapped his wings. She wasn't sure what her brother was trying to tell her.

Kezzie tucked her canoe next to the leeward side of the stone. She wasn't going to leave the high king of Tallahatchia stranded.

High King Alexander knelt on the stone, though he eyed Ezra perched on the prow as if worried the goose would nip him. The glance he flicked over Kezzie didn't seem to hold recognition.

That shouldn't hurt as much as it did. It wasn't like she had been pining over him for the past few years or anything. She didn't even know him. She'd only met him that one time two years ago at Uncle Daemyn's wedding. It hadn't even been a long meeting. He'd bumped into her, they'd shared a look, a spark crackling between them, and she hadn't been able to put that moment out of her mind since.

Back then, he'd been pale and shaky, having just survived a poisoning. Now, he had filled out, his shoulders broader, his muscles more defined beneath the green shirt he wore.

If she'd found herself attracted to him back then, the flutter of attraction only speared deeper now.

A crash came from somewhere behind High King Alexander, followed by a shout.

"I'm sorry, miss, for commandeering your canoe." After tucking the knife into his belt at his lower back, High King Alexander rolled from the rock into the front of her canoe, landing on the front bench as easily as if he'd grown up paddling this stretch of river all his life. "But we need to get out of here."

Ezra honked and flapped, nearly tumbling from the prow. He swiveled his head around and nipped High King Alexander's arm.

"Ezra!" Kezzie shook herself and shoved her paddle into the water. Her brother shouldn't go around biting the high king, even if he'd climbed into the canoe without permission. There seemed to be extenuating circumstances, and she'd been about to invite him into the canoe properly if they'd had more time.

Zeph dove out of the sky, then arrowed between two of the trees. A moment later, there was a shout that turned into something more like a shriek.

Honking from where they had been swimming alongside her canoe, Zeb and Josiah flapped, ungainly, as they sprinted on top of the water. They managed to get into the air long enough to clear the riverbank before they, too, disappeared into the trees after Zeph.

High King Alexander picked up the second paddle, fending off from the rock. He had to lift his paddle extra high to maneuver it up and over Ezra, but her brother hadn't budged an inch. Instead, he fluffed his feathers, as if put out, whenever the high king's paddle dripped on him.

Kezzie swung the canoe to point downriver, back the way she'd come.

High King Alexander dug in his paddle, setting a fast but measured pace. His shirt sleeves pulled taut over the muscles of his shoulders and back. He handled his paddle like he knew his way around a canoe, and she couldn't blame all the thumping of her heart on the exertion of paddling.

Kezzie matched his pace, and their canoe shot downriver, going with the current as they were. Within moments, they'd put some distance between themselves and whoever was chasing the high king.

As they rounded the nearest bend, a honk came from overhead. She glanced up to spot her three brothers flying overhead. At this distance, she couldn't tell them apart, nor could she decipher the meaning behind their honks.

One of the geese slowed, circling overhead. The other two geese continued onward, flying ahead over the river.

High King Alexander glanced up at the geese, but he didn't ask any questions. He seemed inclined to save his breath for paddling, an urgency to his movements. Whatever had happened back there, it must be deadly serious.

Kezzie swallowed and put her own back and shoulders into propelling Falada as quickly as possible. If there was trouble here in Buckhannock, her father and grandfather would need to know about it. As dangerous as it was, they'd have to return to Castle Firlin.

Was this about her brothers' curse? Had King Cassius

somehow set up a trap for them and the high king had stumbled into it? But how would King Cassius have even known she and her brothers would be coming this way?

Only a minute or two after disappearing from sight, a goose soared back from scouting downriver. He landed in the river with a splash so close in front of the canoe that both the high king and Kezzie had to lean hard into their paddlestrokes to turn the canoe before it could hit him.

Zeph—for she could now see the way the white patch curled around his eye—flapped his wings and honked, as if trying to block them from proceeding any farther downriver.

High King Alexander glanced over his shoulder at her. "I think your pet goose is trying—Ow!" The high king shook his hand, leaning away from Ezra.

Ezra glared with his tiny black eyes, as if utterly unrepentant that he'd just bitten the high king. Again.

"Enough with the biting, Ezra." Kezzie turned back to Zeph. "Is there trouble ahead?"

Zeph bobbed his head in a nod, adding a honk as if for emphasis.

Lots of trouble then.

Kezzie trailed her paddle in the water, doing her best to keep the canoe more or less in place, even as the current pushed them farther downstream. What was going on? She and her brothers had just passed this stretch of river, and there hadn't been any trouble then.

Or, at least, they hadn't seen the trouble. A group of warriors could easily have been camouflaged and hiding while they passed by.

"King Cassius." The high king all but growled the name, his fingers flexing on the paddle. "I'm sorry for getting you into this, miss. Drop me off here. They might let you pass them again if I'm not with you."

Maybe, but maybe not. Besides, she wasn't going to risk her brothers by trying to run the gauntlet of King Cassius's men again, now that she knew they were there.

Was King Cassius hunting her and her brothers? Then why had the warriors let them pass peacefully only a few minutes ago?

Or was this a trap for the high king and she was the one accidentally caught in it?

Either way, she and the high king were cut off from Castle Firlin. They couldn't go upriver, nor could they go downriver. And she wasn't about to just turn the high king loose to fend for himself. She might be a princess, but she was also a Rand, and the Rands were loyal to the high king.

High King Alexander was already digging his paddle into the river, preparing to send the canoe toward the far bank.

Kezzie countered his movement with her own paddle, then faced Zeph yet again. "Can we duck up Kawsill Creek?"

Zeph nodded, then swiveled his head to look at Ezra, giving another honk. Ezra gave a honk and a huffy shuffle in return before he awkwardly flopped off the prow of the canoe into the water.

The two geese flapped and sprinted in that bumbling way geese had before they managed to get themselves into the air. While Ezra circled overhead, Zeph headed in the direction of the creek. At least, Kezzie thought it was Zeph. It was hard to tell with them so high in the sky.

The creek was more a stream, dumping into the Buckhannock River around the next bend.

Would King Cassius have more men stationed up the Kawsill Creek?

If this was all a trap for her, then there would be men waiting at that creek to cut her off, figuring that she would try to flee north into the mountains.

But if this was a trap for the high king, then they would have been planning for a man alone and on foot. Without a canoe, High King Alexander would have been either trapped at the Kawsill or forced to attempt to swim it, something that would have slowed him down enough that he would have been easily captured.

At this point, Kawsill Creek was their only option, no matter what sort of ambush King Cassius had planned.

High King Alexander hesitated, then he, too, nodded, as if coming to the same conclusion. He joined her in paddling once again.

Kezzie leaned into her paddlestrokes, shoving Falada across the water, though not as quickly as before. While they needed speed, they also required stealth.

She steered the canoe so that they hugged the north bank. They skirted around a mess of debris formed from an outcropping of boulders and waterlogged tree trunks. As they rounded a rotting root ball, the mouth of the Kawsill opened to their right, the water rippling with the disturbance of the convergence.

Farther downriver, the prow of a birchbark canoe, one much larger than hers, glided across the water, coming into sight as it patrolled crossways to the river, blocking the way. The warrior in the prow held a bow, an arrow already nocked on the string. The warrior behind him wielded a paddle, guiding the canoe forward. More warriors likely filled the rest of the canoe, still hidden behind the bend, and half of them would be armed rather than paddling.

At the moment, the warriors were looking up, their gazes fixed on the goose circling high overhead and honking uproariously.

Would they realize the goose was one of the four who'd flown past earlier, escorting her? Would they take a shot at him? He was currently at the very edge of arrow range, but he would swoop lower if he thought it necessary for a distraction. So much for this trip keeping her brothers safe.

Kezzie dug her paddle in, and High King Alexander matched her movement. The two of them leaned into the turn as the canoe spun, shuddering as the current from the Kawsill struck them.

The muscles in High King Alexander's arms, shoulders, and back strained beneath his shirt as he dragged their canoe up the Kawsill against the current battering them.

Kezzie added her own strength, and between the two of them, her little canoe shot up the stream, the trees closing around them in seconds, hiding them from sight.

Had the warriors seen them? Or had her brother—whichever one it was—managed to create enough of a distraction?

Kezzie scanned the thick stands of trees arching over the stream on either side of them, the undergrowth dipping low toward the water. She and the high king were now within arrow range from either bank, if King Cassius's men were lurking here along the Kawsill.

High King Alexander, too, searched the banks, even as he kept up their rapid pace of paddling.

Neither of them spoke as they glided beneath the trees, the brown water of the stream gurgling white against Falada's prow.

Zeph flapped low over the river, leading the way so far ahead that she only caught glimpses of him at the very straightest sections of the stream. Ezra glided higher overhead, drifting almost lazily as he matched their pace. Josiah and Zeb remained out of sight, likely keeping an eye on the two groups of warriors hunting the Buckhannock behind them.

A minute passed, then two. No Pohatomie warriors jumped out of hiding. No arrows hissed through the air to strike them. The muscles of her back still wound tight and painful, expecting that arrow at any moment.

But as five minutes stretched into fifteen minutes, then half an hour, her tension eased, even as she became aware of the burn in her shoulders, the shake to her arms, from sustaining such a rapid paddling pace.

Were they safe? Did they dare slow down?

Most importantly, what were they supposed to do now that they were up a creek with only a canoe, two paddles, her bow and arrows, and four geese against all the warriors hunting them?

Chapter 5

Keziah

Her muscles aching after the exertion, Kezzie released a long breath. How should she go about telling the high king that she thought it was safe to slow down for a while?

As she opened her mouth, Ezra swooped down through the trees, distinguishable by the gray patch of feathers that spread across the sides of his face and under his beak, breaking up the black of his head and neck.

Instead of landing in the river, he dropped onto the prow of the canoe, his wings battering the high king in the face, his weight rocking the canoe.

High King Alexander sputtered, halting his paddle-strokes so that he could fend off the faceful of feathers.

"Ezra!" Kezzie suppressed her groan, not sure if she wanted to shove her brother into the river or roll her eyes. "Watch your wings!"

Ezra wiggled his tail as he settled once more onto the bracing bar across the prow of the canoe, giving her a look as he did so. Even being a goose couldn't fully curb the attitude endemic to eighteen-year-old adolescents.

"Your geese are well trained." High King Alexander eyed Ezra, resting the paddle across his lap.

Ezra opened his beak, his muscles tensing.

"No. Don't even think about it." Kezzie gave her brother the sternest look she could manage, given she was sadly lacking in practice at sending her brothers looks of any kind. There was no way she was letting Ezra bite the high king for a third time. It wasn't the high king's fault that he didn't know Ezra wasn't an ordinary trained goose.

Ezra snapped his beak shut, fluffing his wings huffily.

High King Alexander leaned back, as if to put more space between himself and the goose. "I've never seen geese listen to their keeper quite this well."

"Did you hear that, Ezra? I'm your keeper. You need to listen to me." Kezzie worked to keep her face stern. How good it felt to actually banter with her brothers. Even after two days of traveling along the river, she still couldn't get used to it. She'd never been able to speak directly to them like this before, nor give them smirks or grins or fake stern glares.

Ezra hissed at her, then shifted so that his tail feathers were squarely in her direction, his head facing away from her.

High King Alexander stared at Ezra another moment before he dipped his paddle into the river once again, setting a more leisurely pace. "I think we're safe for now. I'm sorry about putting you and your geese in danger, but I needed to get away quickly."

The bubbling feeling in her chest at being able to speak with her brothers vanished. She'd put this off as long as possible but no longer. She'd have to open her mouth and have the high king think her quite odd.

Kezzie dropped her gaze to her canoe. "What else could we have done, Falada? We couldn't leave the high king in danger."

High King Alexander's back stiffened, and he swiveled on the bench. "You know I'm—" His gaze landed squarely on her face for the first time since he'd hopped into her canoe. His eyes widened, then his brow furrowed. "Have we met before?"

Another stab right to the heart. To him, she was merely familiar.

Worse, she couldn't even nod to confirm.

His gaze flicked over her face, as if searching for something. Then his posture relaxed. "Oh, right. Daemyn's wedding. You're his niece. Prince Josiah's sister."

Even worse. He only remembered her because of her brother. Not because they'd shared a moment. A moment when her heart had thumped in her chest, and she'd been beyond thankful that she'd plastered on a smile that whole day so that the curse wouldn't count it as an attempt to communicate. She'd even managed a nod for the high king, passing it off to the curse as a bob to the music some of the relatives had been playing.

Then again, she was hardly being fair. He'd met several hundred people that day at Uncle Daemyn's wedding. Why should he remember one girl he bumped into among the whole clan of Rands?

Kezzie let go of her paddle to pat Falada's side. "The high king has a good memory, Falada. But does he remember my name?"

She was the princess of Buckhannock. Wasn't it the

high king's job to know the names of all the kings, queens, princes, and princesses under him?

He'd better. Otherwise she'd have to figure out a way to tell him, and it was always awkward having to introduce herself by talking to an inanimate object.

High King Alexander closed his eyes for a moment. When they snapped back open, he gave her the same warm smile that created dimples in his cheeks and had stirred a flutter in her stomach back when they'd met two years ago. "Princess Keziah, right? I think Prince Josiah called you Kezzie?"

There was no good way to go about answering that. Kezzie picked up her paddle and returned to propelling the canoe upstream once again. One of them had to, and their canoe had been drifting rather dangerously close to the shallow water near the bank. "I don't know about you, Falada, but I'm curious about what the high king is doing in Buckhannock and what happened back there to cause him to go on the run with a girl he hadn't even recognized at the time."

All right, so that was a bit more sarcastic than she'd meant it to be. Too much of her true feelings showing through.

High King Alexander gave her one last, searching look, as if she was a puzzle he was trying to solve, before he faced forward and returned to paddling. He turned his head to speak over his shoulder. "I came to look for Daemyn. I don't suppose he and Rosanna are at Castle Firlin and have simply neglected to send a message that they arrived safely?"

Ezra turned his head to face the high king and gave a mournful honk.

Kezzie swallowed, meeting her brother's gaze. "That's

right, Ezra. None of the family have heard from him or Rosanna either. We're worried."

"I was afraid of that." High King Alexander used his paddle to fend off a branch floating in the stream. "King Cassius said he'd taken care of Daemyn, but I was hoping it was a lie."

Kezzie's stomach twisted. Uncle Daemyn had survived so much in the past hundred years. It didn't seem possible that anyone—even King Cassius—could outfox him.

The high king kept speaking without waiting for her to reply. "Knowing I'd come looking for Daemyn, King Cassius was waiting for me with his men along the banks of the river. He set up an ambush to lure me away from my guards, then he captured me. I managed to get away, but I wouldn't have gotten far if you hadn't come along."

Then this was all a trap for the high king. Kezzie and her brothers had just been unfortunate enough to stumble into it.

But they were also in even more danger. If the Pohatomie warriors realized who she was, then she would be just as much a target as the high king. She would be a valuable captive in a war against Buckhannock...a war King Cassius had essentially already started by attacking High King Alexander on Buckhannock's soil.

And if King Cassius learned about her brothers' curse...

They were in deep trouble no matter what way one sliced it.

Perhaps they would have been safer if they'd stayed in Castle Firlin after all.

"Falada, you deserve all the credit. You carried us quite swiftly away from danger." Kezzie smiled down at her canoe. It had held up well in the strain of the escape, nimble and maneuverable.

Ezra gave a honk and a fluff of his feathers. Probably taking offense that she'd given all the credit to the canoe and not to her brothers for their role in fighting off the high king's pursuers and scouting the river.

"Fine. You and the others also deserve credit." Kezzie glanced from Ezra to where Zeph still kept station overhead, watching for any signs of danger with all of his big brother protectiveness.

High King Alexander leaned slightly away from Ezra before he spoke. "Your geese were quite brave in the attack. They were more effective than guards."

"What do you think, Ezra? Surely the high king's guards will come looking for him?" All they'd have to do was hide until rescue came. Her stomach dropped at another thought. "Unless he fears that all his guards are dead?"

Ezra gave a hiss, likely saying something unflattering about King Cassius.

High King Alexander sent Ezra another look, as if he was still trying to puzzle out how come the goose was replying to the conversation. "I believe my guards are still alive, but I'm afraid they won't come looking. King Cassius used my blood on some kind of cursed handkerchief he'd gotten from a Fallen Fae. Thanks to that handkerchief, King Cassius looks like me right now. I assume he plans to take my place as high king, and it will look better for him if he returns to Castle Eyota surrounded by my guards."

"Surely the high king's guards know him well enough that he can prove who he is." Kezzie kept her gaze focused squarely on Ezra. She was having this conversation with her brother. Not the high king. "He could just march up to them and tell them he's the real high king."

"It wouldn't work. I've seen a curse like this before, and it isn't something to take lightly." High King Alexander's jaw worked, even as he kept up a steady rhythm with his paddlestrokes. "It has a hold over people's minds, making them think they're seeing me. I had one of my guards with me when King Cassius captured me. As soon as the curse was complete, that guard turned on me. Even I nearly believed King Cassius was the high king, and, well, *I'm* the high king. Curses like this are resistible, and perhaps a few of my guards would be able to shake it off. But there's also a good chance King Cassius would have me arrested as an impostor and executed before those few could even do anything about it."

This was even worse than she'd thought. Josiah had come back from that trip to Pohatomie filled with stories about glass slippers and the power they'd had to twist the mind. How could they possibly fight something like that?

Kezzie swallowed, forcing her voice to sound normal. "What do you think, Ezra? King Cassius must be madder than a riled hornet that the high king got away."

"Probably." High King Alexander sighed as he tilted his head to indicate the forest crowding the stream's banks. "He likely has men still looking for me. He can't secure his place as high king until I'm dead and no longer a threat. Speaking of that..." High King Alexander glanced past her, as if checking behind them, before he picked up the pace of his paddling. "We need to keep moving. King Cassius will send men up this creek looking for us, if he hasn't already. We must assume we're being hunted."

Right. Kezzie dug her paddle in, ignoring the ache in her shoulders and arms. While she had done a fair bit of paddling, this kind of sustained pace wasn't something she was used to.

This was a fine barrel of pickled fish they'd found themselves in. She'd set out on this trip to protect her brothers, and instead they were caught up in even more danger.

Still, it wasn't like they could leave High King Alexander to his own devices. It was their duty to do what they could to protect him.

While that trap hadn't been for her and her brothers, that didn't mean her brothers' curse had nothing to do with the situation. Had King Cassius waited to set all of this into motion until her brothers' curse was imminent? The timing was too convenient. Right when High King Alexander needed his strongest allies, they were weakened because of this curse.

What should she do now? Try to circle through the mountains to get back to Castle Firlin? Or stick to the plan and head for the Rand Clan in the mountains?

She'd have to ask what High King Alexander intended to do. He was the high king, after all. In the end, the decision would be up to him.

But not just yet. Right now, they just needed to focus on escaping. They could figure out the rest once they had put more distance between themselves and their hunters.

The sun rose high in the sky, scorching against her skin in the patches of river where the trees didn't offer enough shade. Sweat soon slicked down Kezzie's back and stuck her clothes to her in an uncomfortable fashion.

But she didn't dare beg to slacken the pace, given that the high king wasn't calling for a rest either. His shirt, too, grew dark down the center of his back, a sheen glinting along his hairline.

Kezzie only stopped paddling long enough to dig her canteen and a pouch of dried meat out of her pack. She shared the food and water with the high king—leaving it out in an indication that he should eat it too—though they didn't speak, instead eating as best they could while paddling.

By the time the sunset spread orange fingers across the sky, the ache in Kezzie's muscles had turned into something closer to agony, her rear end hurt, and she was more than ready to stretch her legs.

As the Kawsill curved around another bend, Zeph swooped low and landed on a large boulder next to the river. He gave a honk, jerking his head in a clear order for them to pull into the bank there. A bossy big brother even in goose form.

There was no point in arguing. Kezzie turned Falada in that direction. "Well, Falada, I reckon Zeph found a likely spot to camp for the night."

High King Alexander shot a glance at her, but he matched her movements. "It should be safe enough to camp for the night. The warriors hunting us will be forced to camp too since it will be too dark and dangerous to attempt to travel at night."

Once the canoe tucked into the lee of a boulder, the high king hopped out and tugged the canoe the last few feet to shore. He held it steady for her as she climbed out. Then together, the two of them picked up the canoe and carried it from the river, hiding it among the brush along the bank.

A few large boulders rested in a cluster farther up the shore, further sheltered by a thick stand of pines.

Kezzie trudged up the bank, halted by one of the boulders, and gratefully let her pack fall to the ground. This would be home for the night. She patted the nearest boulder. "I reckon you wouldn't block enough light if we were to light a fire, would you?"

High King Alexander stretched, then glanced around. "I don't think a fire would be advisable. We made good time, but King Cassius's men are likely still too close."

That meant a cold meal and a far colder night.

Especially for the high king. He didn't have anything. Not a pack. Not a spare cloak. Nothing.

Kezzie sighed and patted the boulder again. "I reckon you'll have to do for building a shelter. Or perhaps your friend over there would be better."

High King Alexander sent an assessing look over the boulders before he nodded and pointed at the largest boulder set beneath a spreading spruce tree. "Yes, I think that one would be best. We can build a lean-to against it." He met her gaze, shifting and clearing his throat. "I'm afraid there isn't enough daylight to make two shelters."

Ah. Right. Kezzie hadn't thought of that just yet.

"I can sleep elsewhere. Perhaps under that tree over there." High King Alexander gestured to one of the smaller pines. It had a thick, orange layer of needles beneath it.

Strange as it would be to share a shelter with the high king, she wasn't about to ask him to sleep under nothing but the sparse branches of a scraggling pine. He didn't even have a blanket.

Come to think of it, she might have to share her blanket with him too.

Her face burning, she scrambled to find an object to address. This was fine. It was practical. Nights in the mountains got cold, and since they couldn't make a fire, sharing a shelter and staying warm only made sense.

Her voice slightly strained, Kezzie tried to be nonchalant as she rested a hand on the boulder again, rather thankful to have the excuse to face the rock rather than the high king. "The high king is just being ridiculous, isn't he, Boulder? There is no reason we can't share a shelter."

Both Ezra and Zeph honked. Zeph even waddled up to her and glared at her with his beady black goose eyes.

"What, Zeph? It isn't like we can ask the high king to freeze tonight. He's the high king." Kezzie crossed her arms and glared right back. Her brothers' objections just made her all the more determined. "Besides, it isn't like we won't be properly chaperoned."

High King Alexander's gaze flicked from her to the two geese, then back to her. "I give you my word of honor as the high king. You are in no danger from me."

"Now look what all your overprotectiveness has done." Kezzie kept glaring at her brothers as she waved at the high king. "You made the high king reckon I doubt his honor. As if I'm not perfectly capable of clobbering him a good one if he tried anything. Which I know he won't. Uncle Daemyn wouldn't be his friend if he were that kind of man."

She wasn't even sure why her chest burned with this seething anger. As if she felt the need to rise to the high king's defense.

After one last look at her, Zeph waddled across the small clearing and halted in front of the high king, subjecting him to the same stern glare he'd given Kezzie a moment before.

High King Alexander met her brother's gaze with surprising solemnity for someone who thought he was looking at a mere goose. "If it makes you feel better, I fully expect all of you to pile in between us."

Kezzie gaped at the high king. Had he figured out Zeph

was her brother? Or had he simply come to the conclusion that Zeph wasn't a regular goose of some sort?

"Now that, Zeph, is a sensible plan. It will be warmer that way." Kezzie dragged her gaze away from the high king to smirk at her youngest brother. "All of you are so fluffy now, Ezra, with your lovely goose down feathers. Perfect for cuddling."

Ezra hissed at her, flapping his wings. Even Zeph twisted his head around, his head tilted as if he was trying to give her the goose version of an eyeroll.

Not that she really wanted to cuddle with her brothers, but teasing them was just too much fun, now that she could actually speak to them.

"We should get to work. The daylight is fading fast." High King Alexander stepped around Zeph and drew his long knife from where he'd stashed it when he climbed into her canoe. "I'll cut the saplings. Could you assemble the shelter?"

Kezzie pushed away from the boulder. "Ezra, do you reckon you could help me with that? I'll assemble the main part of the shelter. You can tear off spruce boughs. We'll need lots of those."

Ezra ruffled his feathers, shaking his head.

Zeph honked at him. Ezra honked back, sounding even more like a pouting adolescent reluctant to do any work. Zeph marched over, his webbed feet slapping on the rocky ground, and honked right in Ezra's face.

Ezra's next honk somehow managed to be sarcastic before he hop-flapped over to the nearest spruce tree.

High King Alexander was giving her brothers that assessing look again. After a moment, he shook himself and tromped a few feet into the surrounding forest.

He was destroying all her conceptions of what a high

king should be like. Based on her family's stories, she'd had an image of a handsome but rather useless king when it came to practical skills like using a long knife or paddling a canoe. Their meeting at Uncle Daemyn's wedding had been too short to correct those impressions.

Over the past two years, she'd used those stories to tell herself how foolish her little infatuation was. While she was a princess, she was also a Rand, the daughter of a long line of tough mountainfolk. She shouldn't be attracted to a man who couldn't take care of himself in the mountains.

But as High King Alexander rolled up his sleeves and set to work on some of the saplings a few yards into the forest, Kezzie struggled to tear her gaze away.

Perhaps High King Alexander had once been of the city folk. But he wasn't that helpless high king now. He'd spent too much time with Uncle Daemyn for that.

This high king—the one who held a long knife as if he knew what he was doing, his shirt soaked with the sweat of a hard day's paddle—was a bit too attractive for comfort.

And she was going to have to share a shelter with him that night.

Oh brother.

CHAPTER 6

ALEXANDER

Alex hacked at the base of a small pine tree, the noise loud in the quiet of the evening forest. At least he had one of the larger knives that had come into prevalence in the hundred years while he'd been asleep. It did a better job at chopping down trees than his old dagger would have.

Finally, the tree pitched over, cracking at the base. He had to chop the last section free before he stood. Holding the top of the tree, he sliced off the branches on one side.

Once that was done, he wiped the knife with a rag before he sheathed it. All the tree chopping had done a good job of cleaning off the dried blood from stabbing the Pohatomie warrior and slicing King Cassius's arm, though the knife had gotten sticky with tree sap.

Alex gathered up all the fallen branches. Carrying them in one hand, he dragged the tree back to their camp with his other hand.

Dusk gathered, turning the forest dark and gloomy around them, while a damp chill pervaded the air, hinting of the cold night to come. A hush had fallen over the forest in that twilight state when the birds and insects of the day had gone to sleep and the nighttime frogs hadn't yet set up their chorus.

Beside the designated boulder, Princess Keziah layered spruce branches over their shelter. While Alex had cut down several saplings, she had hauled fallen logs and leaned them against the boulder to form the sturdy frame for their shelter. She'd rested Alex's saplings on top, then used the branches he'd left attached to weave the first layer of spruce branches in place.

He leaned this sapling in the final spot at the end of the shelter with the top by the ground and the cut end resting on the top of the boulder. This faced the branches down in the right way to shed water, should it rain during the night. "I think this is the last one we need."

Princess Keziah didn't so much as acknowledge those words. It might have seemed rude, but she hadn't directly responded to anything he'd said, not even with a nod or a smile. He would have guessed she was uncomfortable around him, but she'd defended him to the geese readily enough.

Geese that acted far too human, much the way Prince Berend did while in his bear form. There was a certain look that humans transformed into animals had. Something about the eyes still shone with the human soul.

Alex knelt, peering inside the shelter. Princess Keziah had built something of a platform out of fallen sticks, which would keep them off the ground. But it still needed to be thickly layered with spruce and pine boughs before it would be even remotely comfortable for the night. "Well done on the logs. Ezra, do you have a few more spruce branches?"

The goose—the one that seemed more sulky than the other one—waddled over with another spruce branch clutched in his beak. He dropped the branch beside Alex, then clacked his beak several times. Pine sap gummed the edges.

Here went nothing. Alex faced the goose as if talking with a person. "I'm sure all that sap doesn't feel great. Perhaps your sister can help you wash it off once we're finished."

The goose gave a honking squawk, flapping his wings as his beak dropped open.

Princess Keziah made a noise in the back of her throat.

Alex lifted his gaze from the goose to her. "It's true, isn't it? I thought it odd, once I realized who you were, that you'd have a pet goose with the same name as one of your brothers. And you called the other one Zeph, which is the same nickname Prince Josiah uses for your oldest brother. Perhaps you wanted to tease your brothers by naming geese after them, but I've been watching. They aren't normal geese, and I've seen the look of a human in animal form before. These are your brothers."

Princess Keziah adjusted one of the spruce branches on the side of the shelter, her gaze dropping to Ezra. "I reckon your secret's out, Ezra. It seems the high king is quick on the uptake."

"I was gifted with intelligence. I try to use it occasionally." Alex hoped his smile came across as self-deprecating. There was a time when he viewed his Loyal Fae gift of intelligence with far too much arrogance. He reached for another branch from the pile Ezra had gathered. "What happened? A curse?"

Ezra bobbed his head in a nod.

"Did King Cassius catch all of you in a curse as well?"

Alex glanced between Ezra and Keziah, searching their faces. How deep did King Cassius's conspiracy go?

Ezra shook his head, hunching as if curling in on himself.

Keziah bent and rested a hand on Ezra's back. "Don't blame yourself, Ezra. It isn't your fault that you're the youngest, and the curse placed on all our brothers is that they would turn into geese on their youngest brother's eighteenth birthday. It sure made for a downer of a birthday a few days ago."

Then this wasn't another curse triggered by King Cassius, but instead it was the curse laid on the four brothers when they were each eight days old.

Still, that didn't absolve King Cassius entirely. It was possible he had learned of the curse and timed his move accordingly.

"Did King Cassius attack you too? Is that why you are out here without any guards?" Alex pushed to his feet and headed for the nearest spruce tree. Ezra had done a good job of stripping off the lower branches, but Alex took out his knife again to slice off the higher ones.

Keziah straightened and fiddled with the branches covering the shelter for a moment before she joined him by the spruce tree. She drew her knife, though she held it in front of her. "The plan went quite awry, didn't it, Conrad?"

Conrad? Was that the name of her knife? She had been calling her canoe Falada earlier in the day.

"We were pretending to be a simple goose girl and her flock." Her gaze still focused on her knife, Keziah gave a shrug. "My idea."

"That's exactly what I thought you were until I finally recognized you." Alex chopped a few more spruce branches off the tree. The pretense explained the lack of guards.

Zeph, the other goose prince present, shot a look at them that Alex couldn't interrupt on the goose's face. After a moment, Zeph faced the forest again, seemingly keeping watch while Alex and Keziah worked.

"I know, Zeph. We were supposed to be heading to the Rand Clan home deep in the mountains where we would be safe." Keziah turned back to the tree and sliced off a branch with her knife. "But we can't blame the high king if things went all wrong."

Alex winced. "I'm sorry for that." He hadn't meant to put her and her brothers in danger.

Keziah huffed as Ezra waddled closer. "The high king is being ridiculous, Ezra. He isn't to blame for King Cassius's actions."

No, but Alex was still the reason King Cassius had invaded Buckhannock. He was the reason Daemyn and Rosanna were currently in danger.

Life would be so much safer for his friends if Alex wasn't the high king.

Wasn't the high king...Alex's hands stilled as the thought churned through him. If King Cassius wanted the throne so badly, how bad would it be to just let him have it? Alex had fought so hard for that throne, and all it had brought him were curses and attempts on his life and misery for his friends.

It would be so much easier to just...leave. Disappear into the wilds of Buckhannock and never give another thought to the broader troubles plaguing Tallahatchia.

Alex shook those thoughts away. He'd been tempted with that false peace before. He wouldn't give in to the temptation now.

Stabbing his now thoroughly sticky knife into the tree, Alex gathered the branches both he and Keziah had cut. He carried them back to the shelter, then laid them out inside.

As he crawled out of the shelter, the pieces clicked into place. "Your brothers' curse was the reason Daemyn and Rosanna planned to be in Castle Firlin."

Trust Daemyn to continue to be circumspect when it came to his family, even with Alex. He hadn't even told Alex what their curse was or that it was about to strike.

Even as he had that thought, a pang shot through him. He met Keziah's gaze where she still worked at chopping more spruce branches. "Daemyn wouldn't miss something as major as your brothers' curse taking effect."

All this time, Alex had been hoping against hope that perhaps whatever had delayed Daemyn and Rosanna wasn't something serious. That King Cassius had been lying.

But Daemyn would move the mountains before he missed being there for his family. He was either dead or in a heap of trouble.

Ezra leaned his neck against Keziah's leg, giving a mournful honk.

Keziah heaved a sigh. "I know, Ezra. Uncle Daemyn promised you he'd be there. He'd never break a promise like that. The whole family is fretting something fierce. Asa and Zeke left to look for him and Rosanna."

"Good. If anyone can rescue Daemyn, it would be Zeke and Asa." Alex tried to breathe easier, but he couldn't quite manage it past the tightness in his chest.

Daemyn and Rosanna could be anywhere in the Buckhannock mountains. Perhaps even in southern Pohatomie, if King Cassius's men had lured or driven them there. With miles upon miles of trackless mountains to search, Zeke and Asa might not arrive until it was too late. If they ever found them.

But what could Alex do about it? He was in just as much trouble at the moment, alone except for Princess Keziah and her four goose brothers, and hunted by King Cassius's men.

He'd have to ponder it. For now, he needed to finish this shelter before it was fully dark.

Chapter 7

Alexander

As the full dark of night closed around them, Alex rubbed his hands together as he and Keziah sat inside the shelter they'd built. It was rudimentary, with a lean-to style roof formed of saplings and covered with spruce boughs. They'd heaped more spruce boughs on the ground to keep them off the cold dirt, then Princess Keziah had spread out her cloak and blanket over the boughs to further cushion them. The oilskin used for protecting her pack in the canoe formed a flap over the open end of the shelter.

Alex studied Princess Keziah in the flickering orange light of the candle she had dug out from her pack and lit. She'd set it on a rock near her where it wouldn't light anything else on fire. Inside the shelter as it was, the small candle's flame wouldn't be visible from that far away, so it was safe enough.

Keziah sat cross-legged on her bedroll at the far end of their shelter, leaning against the boulder they'd used as the back wall of their shelter. Her pack, quiver, and bow leaned against the boulder in the corner.

Despite his protesting honks over Keziah's cuddling comment earlier, Ezra had settled in next to her. Crown Prince Zephaniah remained on guard duty outside while the final two goose princes had yet to return from scouting.

Alex blew on his hands, trying to warm his fingers. He wasn't sure he should bring this up, but he suspected it would be up to him to break the silence. "You never speak directly to me. At first, I thought you might be shy. But you turn to your brothers or the canoe or even a rock whenever you need to answer. I've seen enough curses to recognize the effects of one. It has something to do with the curse you were given when you were eight days old, doesn't it?"

Keziah stiffened, her gaze dropping away from him. After a moment, she rested a hand on Ezra's back. "I said it before, Ezra, the high king is quick on the uptake."

He would take that as a yes, this was her curse.

Ezra lifted his head from where he'd had it tucked under his wing, though he didn't bite Keziah or honk to protest her hand on his back.

Keziah smiled down at the goose prince. "At least I can talk to you, now that you're a goose. That's how my curse works. Animals and objects, but no people."

"Ah." That explained all the random rocks, canoes, and knives. "That's a clever work-around."

The smile dropped from Keziah's face as she continued to meet her brother's gaze rather than look at Alex. When she spoke, her tone was almost bitter. "Clever, he says. Most people call it strange."

Ezra rested his head on Keziah's knee, giving a mournful honk.

"And that's the worst part, Ezra. I'm almost glad you, Josiah, Zeph, and Zeb are geese. For the first time in my life, I can actually talk to you. Isn't that selfish? Here you are stuck as geese, and all I can think about is how glad I am."

Her voice rang with such a depth of pain that something tightened in Alex's chest. She looked so forlorn, huddled against the boulder at the back of their shelter with her black hair tumbling around her shoulders, a lifetime of pain welling in her deep brown eyes.

It must have been so difficult, growing up without ever being able to speak to a person. Not her mother. Not her father. Not her four brothers. No one.

He'd lived a childhood with the burden of a curse. He well knew the pain ringing in her voice.

He found himself leaning forward with the urge to gather her in his arms and let her cry out that ache.

But doing something like that—even in an innocent gesture of comfort—would surely get him bitten by her goose brother. If not soundly thrashed by all four of them.

Alex forced himself to relax back into his seat by the door. "Maybe a little selfish. But I don't think it's a selfishness that your brothers will hold against you. Perhaps, instead, you can think of it as the gift the Highest King is giving you—and them—through this curse."

Ezra lifted his head, giving Keziah a vigorous nod before he bumped her arm.

Keziah blinked down at Ezra for a long moment. "Does that mean you don't hold it against me?"

Ezra gave an even more decisive nod.

With a choked sound in the back of her throat, Keziah gathered Ezra into her arms, squeezing him like he was a toy, stuffed goose.

Ezra honked and squirmed, his black, webbed feet waving uselessly.

"Sorry, Ezra. But I've never been able to hug you before. I'm going to take every chance I get to do it now." Keziah hugged the goose even tighter. "Besides, you're just so fluffy and warm beneath that outer layer of feathers."

Ezra gave another, more affronted honk. After another moment, he nipped her shoulder.

The bite must not have been nearly as hard as the two he'd given Alex earlier in the day, for Keziah just laughed before she set him down. "Fine, fine. That's enough of the aggressive hugging for now. But I'm warning you. There will be more hugs."

Ezra ruffled his feathers as he marched a few feet away from Keziah. He settled down on the blanket well out of her reach.

Alex stifled his own laughter as he buried his cold fingers in the cloak beneath him. Was this what it was like to have siblings? The closest person to a brother he'd had was Daemyn—well, Jadon, back then—and Daemyn had spent their childhoods serving Alex as a manservant. The joking camaraderie hadn't come until the last few years since Alex had woken from his cursed sleep.

His laughter died, the ache returning inside his chest. What if Daemyn was already dead? Had Alex lost his only friend and brother?

Surely not. Surely Daemyn was too wily, too tough, too much mountain born and bred, to have been killed off for the tenth and final time.

Alex cleared his throat, needing a distraction for himself. "If you don't mind me asking, what's your gift?"

Kezzie sighed and rested her hands in her lap. "I don't know about you, Ezra, but I think the Loyal Fae was even more uncreative than the Fallen Fae when dispensing our gifts. All five of us have the gift of good health. We're descended from the mountainfolk. We were already hardy. But none of us have ever had so much as a cold, so I suppose that is convenient."

Especially for her, though she didn't say that out loud. But with her curse, she would have struggled to communicate her illness if she ever became sick.

The *whump* of wings sounded outside before what seemed to be a conversation formed of honks and flapping wings.

After a few moments, goose feet slapped closer. The oilskin moved as a black goose's head pushed inside. The goose glanced around a moment before his body followed his head inside.

Two more geese shoved inside after this first goose.

Alex shifted his legs out of the way to give the geese more room to trundle past him.

The geese lined up in the space between Alex and Keziah, their heads swiveling back and forth as if they weren't sure whom they should face.

Keziah gestured first to the goose on Alex's far left, then worked her way across the three geese. "Welcome to our shelter for the night, Zeph, Zeb, Josiah. The high king figured out who you are, so there's no point in hiding it."

All three of the geese turned and stared at Alex. Zephaniah was faintly familiar, as he'd been with them all day. There was something extra stern about Zephaniah's black eyes as he focused on Alex. Zeb—or Prince Zebediah—was the largest of the geese while Josiah had a faint brown speckling in the white feathers coating his chest and lower part of his body.

"It's good to meet you, Prince Zebediah, though I wish

it were under better circumstances." Alex gave the goose prince a nod, which the goose returned. He turned to goose Josiah, the only one of the four princes he'd met before. "Prince Josiah, you've gained feathers, wings, and webbed feet since the last time I saw you."

Josiah made a noise somewhere between a honk and a hiss. Was that a goose version of a laugh?

Alex sobered and swept his gaze over the four geese and Keziah. "Now that we're all here, we should discuss what we're going to do now."

As much as they could discuss it when Keziah couldn't talk to Alex and none of the geese could talk at all.

"I, for one, am very curious about the high king's plan." Keziah shifted against the boulder, as if trying to make herself more comfortable. She waved to the still sulking Ezra. "What about you, Ezra?"

Ezra gave a honk, bobbing his head.

Zephaniah, Zebediah, and Josiah found spots around Keziah's side and legs, all of them facing Alex. After a moment, Ezra joined them, though he gave Keziah a stern look as if ordering her to refrain from hugs.

Alex eyed all of them, trying to ignore the wafts of cold air drifting around the oilskin flap. Would they mind if he joined that goose pile at the back of the shelter? Right now, he would gladly hug one of Princess Keziah's goose brothers if it meant staying warm.

Shoot, he'd even snuggle up with Rosanna's brother Berend in his bear form. Surely with all that fur, he'd be nice and warm.

Another pang twisted the knot of worry in his chest. Perhaps he should have given in to Berend's pleading and let him come along. It sure would have been nice to have a black bear on his side right about now.

But Alex had asked Berend to stay behind, continuing his duties as Neskahana's representative on the King's Council.

Alex shoved his thoughts and worries away. He focused on Prince Zephaniah. "Here's the situation as I see it. King Cassius set this whole plot in motion, using your curse to trap Daemyn, using Daemyn to trap me, and finally using a magical handkerchief to take my place as high king. And right now, the six of us are the only ones in Tallahatchia who know the full scope of his plot."

The four geese nodded. Keziah didn't react at all, but Alex hadn't expected her to, given that her gaze rested on him.

"We need to get word of what is happening to your grandfather or to someone in the Rand Clan who can pass a message to him." Alex held up a hand, ticking off their goals with his fingers. "We also need to rescue Daemyn, evade our pursuers, and stop King Cassius from taking the throne of the high king."

Even as he said it, the weight of the situation sat heavily on Alex's shoulders. How was he supposed to even accomplish one of those things when his only allies were four princes transformed into geese and a princess who couldn't talk to people?

Not to mention his own lack of skills. He'd come a long way in the past three years, but he still didn't have the depth of knowledge of someone mountain born, like Daemyn.

The others watched him intently, as if still waiting for him to come up with a plan. It would be great if his gift of intelligence kicked in right about now. He sure could use something exceptionally clever to get them out of this mess.

Alex reached past the oilskin, patted the ground for a moment, and swept up a handful of pebbles. After smoothing out a section of the blanket laid over the spruce boughs, Alex held up one of the pebbles. "This is us." He placed the pebble at the edge of his smoothed area closest to Keziah and the geese. "Castle Firlin is somewhere over here while the Rand Clan is over there." He set two more pebbles spaced far to the edges of his makeshift map.

The geese stretched their necks out, tilting their heads as they studied the pebbles.

"If I were to guess, I'd say Daemyn and Rosanna are somewhere to our northeast, boxed in by a third band of Pohatomie warriors." Alex added one pebble for Daemyn and Rosanna, then a second one for the enemy warriors. He added yet more pebbles in a line with Castle Firlin, farther south than the pebble that designated him, Keziah, and the geese. "We know there is a band of Pohatomie warriors on the Buckhannock between us and Castle Firlin. Another band between us and the river going the other way."

King Cassius had deployed quite the force in Buckhannock between those three bands, and that was assuming there weren't more Pohatomie scouring the forest that Alex didn't yet know about.

King Cassius's men had likely been reinforced by the Tuckawassee who'd left their own kingdom, due to their queen's loyalty to the high king.

The largest goose, Zebediah, heaved himself to his feet and waddled closer to the map. Stretching out his neck, he nudged the pebbles for the two bands of Pohatomie warriors with his beak until they knocked together. He then rolled the two of them slightly north, as if they were following the same creek as Alex and Keziah.

"Are you telling me that the two bands of Pohatomie joined into one and are following us?" Alex gestured to the pebbles.

Zebediah nodded before he waddled back to his place next to Keziah, settling down once again by her feet.

That made for quite the force on their tail. Perhaps the large group wouldn't be able to move quite as quickly as a small party.

Then again, these were trained warriors with multiple paddlers per canoe while Alex and Keziah were royalty who weren't at quite the same level of fitness. It would be a challenge to keep their lead.

Alex shook that thought aside for now. He held up a particularly misshapen, manure-colored pebble. "Did either of you see if King Cassius joined my guards?"

This time, it was Josiah who honked, nodded, and rose to his webbed feet.

Alex set the ugly pebble on the blanket, adding a second pebble to designate his men. "Are they heading for Castle Eyota? Could you tell?"

Josiah nodded, then sprinted a few steps, as if in a hurry.

As Alex had suspected, King Cassius had hightailed for Castle Eyota to solidify his claim to the throne, leaving his men to deal with Alex. "After the attack, my guards were probably more than happy to turn around to get 'me' back to safety as quickly as possible."

After a moment, Josiah flapped his wings and honked, as if he was trying to tell Alex something more. He jabbed his beak toward the ugly, King Cassius pebble.

When Alex stared at him, still uncomprehending what the goose was attempting to tell him, Josiah turned to

Keziah and tapped his beak against her foot in what seemed to be a pattern.

Was it the Rand family code? Even after all these years, Alex had yet to learn it. Daemyn might teach him, if he asked. But Alex had decided not to do so, instead leaving this part of Daemyn's life as his own.

Keziah tilted her head, as if listening to something. "Josiah, you saw King Cassius, and he looked like the high king. But only briefly before you saw beneath the curse."

Josiah bobbed a nod, more vigorously this time. He ruffled his feathers almost indignantly.

"You know the truth. You've also had more practice than most with curses of this sort." Alex met Josiah's goose eyes, his mouth tilting in a wry smile at the memories of that trip to Pohatomie and the glass slippers.

"At least there's a way to see beneath this curse." Keziah focused on her brother, not on Alex. "That's good news for the high king."

"It is. Though it's possible that Josiah's previous experience with curses and his being a goose have something to do with his ability to see through this current curse's effects." Alex sighed and ran a hand over his face. "If this is anything like the curses I've seen before, then the curse will have more of a hold over people the longer they are with King Cassius. Only a very few will be able to shake it off."

Did that mean Alex would be better off confronting King Cassius sooner rather than later? The longer Alex waited, the more people King Cassius would have under the power of this curse.

Keziah must have had similar thoughts, for she leaned forward and picked up the pebble standing in for their group. She hopped the pebble in a circle through what would be the mountains until it reached the King Cassius pebble. "Little pebble, perhaps you should sneak through the forest like this and surprise that nasty King Cassius before he gets farther away."

As much as Alex wanted to rush after King Cassius and wrest his men away from the scheming king, there was every chance Alex's men would turn on him. Nor could he risk a fight where his own men might be killed fighting each other.

Alex sighed and shook his head. "King Cassius will have the benefit of sticking to the established trails and waterways. I don't think we could possibly catch up to him, much less get to Castle Eyota before he does. Even if I got word to Castle Eyota to send out my army to stop him, the army would just as likely end up under the power of the curse. I don't like the idea of letting him gain a foothold in Castle Eyota, but I don't have a choice. I need to gather my allies—allies I know won't be taken in by the curse—before I confront him."

Alex needed Daemyn. He and Rosanna were some of the few Alex could trust not to be taken in by this curse.

Alex's mother wouldn't be taken in either, but she was living at the far eastern side of Kanawhee with her new husband and stepchildren. Alex could ask her, her husband, and her husband's warriors to come, but he wasn't close enough with his stepfather to wish to bring them into this trouble if he didn't have to. His mother deserved her peaceful new life after all the loss and tragedy she'd endured the past few years.

"I'd still like to send word to the King's Council at Castle Eyota. Even if they can't move against King Cassius, they can at least prepare for his arrival." Alex returned his pebble back to its position up the creek.

If he warned them, the King's Council, at least, could

leave the castle and go into hiding before King Cassius arrived. That way, King Cassius might hold the castle, but the true government of Tallahatchia wouldn't be fully under his control.

Alex rolled the last pebble around in his fingers before he set it alongside the one for the Rand family. "King Cassius will be hounding my footsteps, but if we split up, there is a good chance the warriors will leave Princess Keziah alone, especially if they haven't realized who she is yet. I think you should make for the Rand Clan as you originally planned. You'll be safe there."

The four geese swiveled their heads to look at each other, honking as they seemed to have a conversation among themselves.

Keziah's gaze latched onto them, even as she crossed her arms with an almost mulish look. "I know what you're thinking, Zeph, and I'm not doing it. Maybe the warriors haven't realized who I am, but there's a good chance they have. At the very least, they have to be growing suspicious about the rather too intelligent geese that have been hanging around. If we head for the family, we could be bringing King Cassius's men right to their doorstep. They're a tough lot, but they're a peaceful bunch. A lot of women and children. I won't put them in danger. It was one thing to hide among them when King Cassius didn't know where we were or what we were doing. It's another thing when we might have given ourselves away."

Zephaniah ruffled his feathers, then, slowly, bobbed his head.

As much as Alex wanted to send Keziah to safety, she made a rather good point. He'd never forgive himself if King Cassius's men wiped out Daemyn's extended family because of Alex.

"Besides"—Keziah's dark brown eyes flashed—"We can't leave the high king on his own. He's our responsibility now. Uncle Daemyn would want us to do nothing less than our best to protect him."

Zephaniah gave something that was almost a sigh, if a goose could do such a thing. Zebediah and Ezra swung their heads to regard Alex with black eyes while Josiah bobbed his head and made that honk-hiss laughing sound.

Alex opened his mouth to argue before he closed it on a sigh of his own. "I greatly appreciate your loyalty. While Daemyn has done his best to teach me survival skills, I'm afraid I don't have the training to navigate the mountains by myself."

"See." Keziah's mouth tipped in a smile as she gestured to Alex, her gaze still on Zephaniah. "We can't let the high king get lost in our mountains. What kind of Rands would we be?"

Josiah honked and stretched his neck like he was cheering. Ezra bumped his head against Keziah's hand. Both Zephaniah and Zebediah gave bobs of their heads.

"Thank you." Alex swept his gaze over the gathered geese and princess. They were a motley bunch, and paltry in number compared to what he was facing. But he was grateful to have them on his side anyway. Loyalty counted for a great deal right now.

Loyalty. Like Daemyn's loyalty, which had carried him all the way to the threshold of Beyond and through the hundred years of peril and deaths. A loyalty that Daemyn was once again paying for. Hopefully not with his or Rosanna's life.

What should Alex do now? He squeezed his eyes shut and forced himself to take long, slow breaths.

As the high king, the Lord of All Fae and Men had

given him a duty to rule over Tallahatchia. He could not abdicate that duty by being reckless with his life.

By that logic, he should do all in his power to reach Castle Firlin. He should stay behind those walls while Zeke, Asa, and King Omri's warriors combed the mountains to search for Daemyn and Rosanna.

That was what he should do. But what he *wanted* to do? He wanted to set out into the mountains and rescue Daemyn and Rosanna from whatever trap King Cassius had devised.

Was it hubris to think he could save Daemyn? This was *Daemyn*. If he'd gotten himself caught, then it must have been one skillful trap indeed.

Besides, who was Alex to think that *he* should be the one to rescue Daemyn? Zeke and Asa had already set out to look for him. No one, except perhaps Daemyn himself, was more capable.

Alex should leave Daemyn and Rosanna's safety in their hands. He should choose the crown over his friends. Shouldn't he? Would he be utterly foolish if he set off into the mountains to do all in his power to rescue them instead of rescuing his kingdom?

Daemyn and Rosanna were his family, the only family he had besides his mother. Well, he had his stepfather and stepsiblings, but with his title of high king as a barrier, they weren't close. They were more his mother's second family than his.

But Daemyn had sacrificed so much, done so much, and risked so much for Alex over the years. Alex owed him everything.

What would the Highest King have him do? He tried to clear his mind and search his heart for a nudge. A breeze whispered across his face, but he didn't feel that same peaceful reassurance he'd felt when making other big decisions. No clear answer as to what he should do.

Perhaps this was a time when the Highest King would use wise counsel to show Alex the right decision. Alex didn't dare lean on his own understanding and feelings right now.

He faced Keziah and her four brothers. "The way I see it, we have two options. Either we circle through the mountains to Castle Firlin and wait there for your grandfather's warriors to clear out King Cassius's men. Or..." Alex let the pause linger as he met each of their gazes. "We set out to rescue Daemyn and Rosanna ourselves."

The geese broke out into a flurry of honks and wing flaps. Something of an argument seemed to break out with Zephaniah and Zebediah facing Josiah and Ezra. Josiah's honks were the most strident, and he repeatedly tapped his beak on the stone representing Daemyn and Rosanna. One guess what his opinion was. Still the adventurous one, even in goose form.

Keziah's eyes narrowed as she studied first the map, then her brothers, then Alex, as if she was waiting to speak until she'd assessed everything.

"Heading to Castle Firlin is the safer choice. But if we do that, Daemyn and Rosanna will be left in danger even longer." Alex didn't add that they might not survive long enough for warriors from Castle Firlin to rescue them. "I know Zeke and Asa already have a head start in searching for them. But we have a winged advantage they don't have. With the four of you scouting by air, we'll be able to cover far more territory. Not to mention, we know *why* Daemyn and Rosanna are missing. Zeke and Asa don't. They might even walk into the trap as well."

Alex probably shouldn't be arguing so hard for the

option he personally wanted. He'd asked the opinion of the others so he wouldn't be swayed by his feelings.

But deep in his heart, he wasn't sure he could follow any other option, even if it was the wiser one. Was that the prompting of the Highest King? Or his own personal feelings?

"We can send a message to Castle Firlin to alert your grandfather about what is happening. He can send out additional messages to my allies at Castle Eyota and to the Rand Clan." Alex held Keziah's gaze, knowing she wouldn't like this part of his suggestion. "Keziah, perhaps you could take the message there?"

Zephaniah honked and tapped his beak on Keziah's knee. Perhaps he agreed with Alex on this one.

Keziah's mouth pressed into a tight line, her crossed arms going stiff again, as she dropped her gaze to her brothers. "No, I won't sit safe at Castle Firlin while all of you go off with the high king to rescue Uncle Daemyn and Rosanna. I'm a Rand just as much as the rest of you." She patted her bow and quiver. "And I'm not helpless."

"You aren't a warrior either." Alex spoke quietly. Given that fiery glint in her eyes, she might just turn that bow and arrows on him.

If something happened to her, he'd probably lose the support of Buckhannock. Not to mention that Daemyn and his entire extended family would never forgive him. That wasn't a burden he wanted to carry.

Yet she was a grown woman. He couldn't stop her from coming along either. She was likely more than capable of taking care of herself in these mountains. Far more than he was, after all. If anyone should be sitting behind thick, protective walls, it was him.

Zephaniah's honk held more of an angry hiss to it as he glared at his sister nose to beak.

She glared right back, every inch a stubborn, mountain princess.

Finally, Zephaniah gave a honk, flapped his wings, and waddled to put his tail to Keziah.

She grinned with all the triumph of a little sister getting her way. "I reckoned you'd see it my way if you thought about it long enough."

Zephaniah ruffled his feathers, his back still to her.

"Then if you won't take the message, perhaps one of your brothers can fly it to Castle Firlin?" Alex waved to them.

Keziah reached out and tapped Josiah on the head. "No, don't even think about it. We're not splitting up. Father told me to watch out for the four of you. I know geese are strong and capable of protecting yourselves, but you're still geese. You look like a mighty fine meal to any hunters that might be roaming these hills." She leaned forward and tapped the blanket ahead of the stone representing them on the makeshift map. "If I'm remembering correctly, there should be a village somewhere north of us. What do you think, Zephaniah? Will they have carrier pigeons and message runners?"

For a long moment, Zephaniah remained as he was, stiff and ignoring his sister. Then he unbent somewhat and gave a sharp nod.

"Good. They can send the message to Grandfather." Keziah dug a pinecone out of the spruce branches and placed it on the map. "We'll need to warn them about the Pohatomie warriors regardless."

Alex nodded. It seemed no matter what they did, they'd bring danger to the backwoods people of Buckhannock. Even if they bypassed the village, the Pohatomie warriors wouldn't. They'd raid the town to question them.

Better to visit the town and warn them. The villagers could pass the word to other nearby towns.

"Then it's settled. Whatever we do, we'll do it together." Alex held each of their gazes again. "And I think we are all in agreement on what that should be?"

Josiah gave an enthusiastic honk before he tapped his beak on the pebble for Daemyn and Rosanna.

"I agree with you, Josiah." Keziah leaned forward and tapped Daemyn and Rosanna's pebble as well. "Uncle Daemyn needs our help."

Ezra shuffled forward, and he, too, tapped the pebble.

Zebediah glanced at Zephaniah before he tapped the pebble with his beak.

All of them turned to Zephaniah, staring at him.

With a honk and a flap of his wings, Zephaniah added his vote, tapping Daemyn and Rosanna's pebble.

"It's decided. In the morning, we'll set out to rescue Daemyn and Rosanna." As peace washed through Alex, loosening that knot in his chest for the first time, he leaned forward and rested a finger on the pebble.

Perhaps this wasn't the smart choice. But it felt like the right one.

Daemyn had rescued Alex countless times before. It was time Alex returned the favor.

"I don't know about all of you geese, but I'm going to get some sleep." Keziah reached for the candle set on the rock. "We have an early morning tomorrow."

"Yes. We'll need to keep moving to stay ahead of the Pohatomie warriors." Alex picked up the pebbles and pinecone from the blanket.

Zephaniah honked, his head swiveling between his

brothers as he did so, before he turned and waddled toward the oilskin flap to outside.

Alex held out a hand, stopping the goose from exiting. "I can take a shift at watch."

"Me too, Zeph. Don't you dare leave me out of the watch rotation." Keziah held the flat rock and candle in both hands.

She had a point. If there was anyone Alex would exempt from watch, it would be eighteen-year-old Ezra, not Keziah. Alex lowered his hand to allow Zephaniah to exit. "It would only make sense. With six of us, we can set three watches a night. That means we would all get a full night's rest every other night. With how hard and fast we'll be traveling—and how many miles you'll need to fly to scout—we'll all need rest."

Zephaniah swiveled his head to look at Alex, then at Keziah. After a moment, he nodded. He honked as he motioned to the other geese with his beak.

Josiah waddled to join Alex and Zephaniah by the door while Zebediah shuffled closer to Keziah and Ezra.

"Very well. Josiah, you, and I will be the watches for tonight. Keziah, Zebediah, and Ezra will take tomorrow night." It was a sensible division for the two sets of watches. Alex eyed Zephaniah. "I can take the middle watch."

Zephaniah shook his head quite emphatically before jabbed a beak at Josiah. Josiah honked back and ruffled his feathers.

"All right, fine." Alex wasn't going to argue too hard if Zephaniah wouldn't let the high king take the middle watch—the worst watch of the night since one's sleep was broken into two small stretches. Alex jabbed a finger at

Josiah. "Don't forget to wake me for my watch. No trying to be heroic and taking two watches."

Josiah gave that ruffled feather gesture again, as if in some sarcastic reply.

"Now can we go to sleep?" Keziah rolled her eyes at Zephaniah, holding the candle closer to her mouth as if preparing to blow it out.

Zephaniah honked at her before he waddled into the night.

Keziah made a sarcastic honking sound right back at him before she blew out the candle, plunging the shelter into darkness.

Alex blinked at the blackness. After a moment, his eyes adjusted enough that he could just make out shadowed shapes in the gloom. Some faint moonlight filtered around the oilskin and a few spots around the spruce boughs of the shelter.

The blanket lifted a moment before Keziah wiggled underneath it, stretching out alongside the boulder. Zebediah, Josiah, and Ezra settled next to her, putting themselves between Alex and Keziah.

Well chaperoned, indeed. He'd have to hope he didn't roll too much in his sleep or he'd wake rather suddenly from a goose bite.

Alex shifted until he could tug the cloak over himself, the bed of spruce boughs only marginally more comfortable than the ground. It was scratchy, a bit sticky, and not all that warm. Keziah's cloak was meant for someone of shorter stature, and he had to tuck his moccasined feet in tighter than was comfortable to fit all of him beneath it. But it was the best he'd get for tonight.

As he closed his eyes and willed his body to fall asleep, he had to suppress a snort. There was a time he had turned up his nose at spreading out his blanket on soft hay in a perfectly sound barn or eating a hot stew made of some mystery rodent.

Look at him now. Here he was huddled under pine boughs, not even a blanket or a pack to his name. His stomach still pinched after the unsatisfying dried meat they'd gnawed on for both lunch and supper that day.

He'd have to tell Daemyn about this, once it was all over. They'd get a laugh at how tough Alex was now, compared to what he'd been a few years ago. Or a hundred years ago, depending on how one wanted to look at it.

Daemyn had to be all right. He'd survived a hundred years of both the Tuckawassee and the Pohatomie trying to kill him. Actually, they had succeeded in killing him multiple times. He just hadn't stayed dead since the Highest King had more work for him to do.

Once again, Alex would have to trust Daemyn's and Rosanna's lives to the Highest King.

They'd have to hold on just a little longer. Rescue was on its way.

CHAPTER 8

DAEMYN

In the gray of predawn, Daemyn slid into the shadow cast by a spruce tree, his moccasins whispering across the sandy ground. He eased forward to peer between the undergrowth at the camp sprawling before him.

The Pohatomie camp stretched from one rock wall to the other on both sides of the creek, fully blocking the end of the dead-end gully. Sturdy lean-to shelters formed of logs and spruce branches created a permanence to the camp that hadn't been there nearly two weeks ago when this standoff started. A makeshift bridge had even been constructed over the creek.

Embers glowed in the campfires, burning low after the long night. Yet even as nothing but embers, the campfires still cast enough light that sneaking past them would be difficult. They were spaced across the gully so that no large patches of shadows were left, not even around the log shelters.

Four guards hid behind trees and various boulders, their eyes scanning the darkness where Daemyn hid. Two of the warriors were Pohatomie with their blond hair and pale skin. But the other two were Tuckawassee with jewels gleaming in their thick black hair and in strands over their dark skin.

Daemyn and Rosanna might have been able to evade this war party, except for the enemy that slept in the shelter on the far side of the camp, well away from Daemyn's reach.

Colonel Beshko, the Tuckawassee warrior who seemed to have a particular vendetta against Daemyn. After Daemyn and Rosanna slipped out of her grasp when she'd sprung her trap north of Castle Firlin, she'd pursued them with an almost ruthless relentlessness.

Daemyn eased an arrow from his quiver, slowly nocking it to the string.

The guards were, wisely, hiding behind cover, having learned from previous attacks. But someone had left a shirt to dry next to one of the fires, propped up on a couple of sticks.

Daemyn raised his bow, aimed, and released. The arrow whistled through the still morning air before it struck one of the sticks with enough force to snap it.

The shirt and other two sticks toppled into the fire with a burst of ashes and smoke.

"He's here! He's—" In his urgency to call the warning, one of the guards partially stepped from cover.

Daemyn whipped out another arrow, nocked, drew, and released.

The guard went down with a howl, clutching at the arrow in his leg.

As more warriors spilled from the shelters, strapping on their weapons as they went, Daemyn whirled and dashed back into the forest carpeting the floor of the gully.

Even as he ran, he kept his steps light, dodging between the trees and ducking under branches to leave as little trace of his passing as possible.

Not to mention, he had to avoid all the traps he'd set. This patch of forest was littered with traps, snares, hidden spikes, and anything else he could think to do to dissuade the Pohatomie and Tuckawassee warriors from setting foot deeper in the gully.

He ducked underneath a branch that was really a snag for a swinging log, then leapt over a snare set to hoist someone off their feet.

After another few minutes, he slowed, pausing behind a tree to listen.

At the far end of the gully, the small waterfall roared as it tumbled down the cliff and into the creek at the bottom.

A scream came from the direction of the enemy camp, then another shout. Both of them were distant, and he couldn't hear any other crashing or thrashing of pursuit.

His traps were working.

Daemyn set out at a slower pace, taking a roundabout route through the gully. He set a few more traps and checked his snares, finding a grouse in one of them. Once he was satisfied that the gully was as secure as he could make it, he headed for the path to the cave.

The cave carved into the upper reaches of the gully, only reachable by a thin trail that wound upward in the sandstone in almost step-like ridges.

At the base of the steps, he gave a mourning dove's call, cooing five times in a way that would be rather distinctive.

After a moment, the answering call with four coos answered him.

Giving one last glance over his shoulder, Daemyn hurried up the trail, crouching to make himself less of a target. While the openness of the trail made it easier to defend, it also made Daemyn vulnerable. He had to pick his way around the various triggers and traps he'd set up. One wrong footstep, and he'd set off a rockfall.

As he ducked into the cave, Rosanna set aside her slingshot and wrapped her arms around him. "You're back."

"Safe and sound." Daemyn kissed her temple, holding the grouse well away from her as he embraced her with his other arm.

Rosanna pulled away, sweeping a glance over him as if searching for additional bloodstains.

"As I said, safe and sound." Daemyn forced a lighthearted smile as he strode deeper into the cave.

The cave curved in the sandstone cliff, its floor an uneven patchwork of slopes and larger rocks. Several openings in the side looked out over the valley, though only one had anything but a sheer drop beneath it. At one end, a trickle from the same stream that fed the waterfall dribbled down the rocks into a basin, forming a pool of fresh water.

Near one of the openings, a small fire smoldered, a stack of firewood next to it. Daemyn would have to go out and fetch more wood soon, though there was enough to cook the grouse.

"All quiet here?" Daemyn knelt on the far side of the entrance, the spot in the cave they had designated for the unpleasant task of gutting animals. He drew his long knife as he set the grouse on the stone floor.

"Yes." Rosanna returned to her seat on the other side of the entrance, and she turned her face toward the valley rather than watch him work.

He didn't mind. She already didn't like watching the gutting process, but especially now that she grew nauseous more easily. He would gladly take care of the dirty work for her.

Her face still turned away from him, she asked, "How are things looking out there?"

"They're even more entrenched at the end of the valley." Daemyn set to work gutting and plucking the grouse. "There ain't a way past them."

Nor was there any other way out of the valley. The cliffs were steep. Perhaps Daemyn could have climbed his way out of there, though he would have been risking his neck to do so. One slip would send him tumbling to his death. But Rosanna didn't have the strength or skills to even think about attempting it.

And right now, with the life she'd also be risking...

They'd decided it was too dangerous. But if they didn't find a way out of here soon, perhaps they would become desperate enough to chance it.

If only they still had their rope. But their rope, canoe, and nearly everything else had to be abandoned when they were ambushed by the band of Pohatomie and Tuck-awassee warriors and made a run for it. They'd only saved the packs on their backs.

The cave had provided a sanctuary, but it was also a trap. They couldn't get out past the Pohatomie and Tuck-awassee. They couldn't get out another way. They couldn't even light a fire where it would be seen by someone from Daemyn's family to alert them to their trouble.

Pausing in his work, Daemyn gestured toward the trail. "I set a few more traps and deadfalls."

"That'll make them think twice before they blunder closer again." Rosanna's hand came to rest over her abdomen, almost as if she made the gesture subconsciously. "But it won't hold them off forever, will it?"

"Reckon not." Those words weighed so heavily he nearly couldn't speak them. "Rosanna..."

"No, don't." Despite her dislike of the blood and guts, Rosanna glanced at him, her brown eyes fierce. "Don't blame yourself. I knew you were a target when I married you. It's King Cassius's fault that he's decided to make trouble again."

Daemyn couldn't hold her gaze. Instead, he busied himself gathering up the feathers and guts and tossing them over the side of the cliff.

Perhaps King Cassius was the one to blame. But that didn't make it any easier to swallow that Rosanna—that their child—was in danger because of Daemyn.

Daemyn gathered up the meat and stood. "I still ain't pleased you got roped into this."

After one glance around the valley, Rosanna shifted so that she could more easily switch back and forth between looking at Daemyn and glancing around the valley. "I'm not happy about it either, but we'll get through this, one way or another."

She sounded so determined to believe that. If only he could believe it too.

Daemyn piled kindling on the ashes of the fire. With the sun rising brighter into the sky, a fire wouldn't be visible, and they'd put it out long before nightfall. Even though the enemy knew where they were, they couldn't risk making it easy for them by skylining themselves against a lit cave.

Once a flame flickered into life, and he'd added a few logs, Daemyn sat back on his heels, his heart heavy as a stone in his chest, and met Rosanna's gaze. "It ain't looking good, Ro. Sure, the Pohatomie and Tuckawassee ain't about to sneak up on us. But we ain't getting out neither.

Sooner or later, they'll get bored just setting there. We can't hold 'em off forever."

Rosanna pushed away from the wall, strode across the cave, and crouched next to Daemyn. She wrapped an arm around him, resting her head on his shoulder. "The mountain speech is coming through thicker in your voice. When it becomes thick as maple syrup, then I know we're in trouble."

He couldn't quite make himself meet her gaze or respond to her attempt at levity.

Rosanna squeezed him in a side-hug, her hand on his arm tightening. "I've traveled to all seven kingdoms of Tallahatchia at your side. We've faced danger, death, waterfalls, river pirates, vengeful kings and queens, and too many curses to name. Facing peril at your side is nothing new. We've always come through before, and I trust the Highest King that we will again. I don't believe this is the end the Highest King has for us. Especially now."

Her hand dropped to her abdomen again, cradling the life there.

Daemyn's stomach twisted, and he looked away. He knew all too well that there were no guarantees. It was entirely possible that the Highest King had given them this new life only to snatch it away. In his hundred years of life, Daemyn had walked through that sorrow with his nieces and nephews many times before.

Despite his trust in the Highest King, it still twisted something bitter inside him.

After two years of marriage, their dreams had begun to be almost painful. A dream of a family of their own. Of seeing his family welcome his children into the fold. They'd hoped and longed and begged the Highest King, only to fear that it was his will that they would never have a child.

When Zeke and Isi had announced they were expecting, Daemyn had been happy for them, but in private he'd held Rosanna while she cried with the mix of joy and pain and seeing her best friend so happy while her arms were still empty. That had spurred them to take this trip, needing some space to clear their heads and hearts by communing with the Highest King.

Now Rosanna was finally pregnant, right when their enemies were closing in.

And there was nothing Daemyn could do to protect his wife and child besides lay a few traps and shoot a few arrows. Eventually—perhaps not today, maybe not even tomorrow—Colonel Beshko would find a way through his gauntlet. Daemyn's skills wouldn't be enough.

"Daemyn." Rosanna lightly rested her hand on his cheek before she turned his face toward her. "Look at me. Don't despair. Don't go there. I need you to believe we will survive just as firmly as I do."

Daemyn released a long breath, squeezing his eyes shut for a moment. He had despaired before, at the end of the hundred years of Alex's curse. It hadn't been right then, and it wasn't right now, no matter how natural such doubts were.

He needed to trust the Highest King. Whatever happened would be for his and Rosanna's good. More, their end was already painted in the Halls of the Lord of All. There was nothing Colonel Beshko or all of the warriors in Pohatomie could do to change it.

Rosanna shook him slightly. "Someone is bound to figure out something is wrong when we don't show up where we're supposed to. I know your family. Someone will come hunting us. And when they do, we'll be able to get out of here. We just need to hold on until then."

Her words banished the last of the despair. Asa and Zeke would scour all of Tallahatchia until they found him. As would Zephaniah, Zebediah, Josiah, and Ezra, even if they were probably geese at this point. And once they rallied the entire Rand Clan, nothing and nobody would stand in their way.

Then there was Alex. Once upon a time, Daemyn wouldn't have trusted him to lift a finger on his behalf.

But now, he was family too. And he'd rally Tallahatchia to save Daemyn.

Daemyn speared the grouse carcass on a spit, then placed it over the fire. When he finally looked up, a smile creased his face. "Reckon you're right. My family ain't about to take it lightly that we've disappeared."

"Exactly." Rosanna grinned before she pressed a kiss to his cheek. "The last time your family rallied to your rescue, they blew up a castle. I can't wait to see what they do this time."

Queen Tamya of Tuckawassee was still rebuilding Castle Greenbrier's outer wall after that incident.

Daemyn's family would come for him. He and Rosanna just needed to survive long enough.

KEZIAH

Kezzie woke to a goose nipping her ear. She lunged awake, rubbing her ear as she glared. "What was that for?"

Standing in front of her face, Josiah extended his neck and honked, eyeing her as if expecting her to understand.

She blinked at the sliver of sky she could see through the partially open oilskin. The sky had barely lightened to gray, the sun not yet peeking over the horizon. "Is it time to get going already? It's awful early."

Josiah honked, bobbed his head in a nod, and flapped his wings as if frustrated that it took her this long to get up.

Beside her, Ezra lifted his head from where it had been tucked under his wing. He hissed at Josiah, shuffling as if he wanted to go back to sleep.

As if finally satisfied that they were awake, Josiah waddled back outside.

The rest of the shelter was empty. The others, including High King Alexander, must already be up. Her cloak was already folded, sitting neatly at the foot of the place where the high king had slept.

In the close confines of the shelter, she'd felt the vibrations through the spruce boughs beneath them every time he tossed and turned, setting up a powerful rustling. The sound of his breathing only a handful of feet away from her was strangely intimate, lying side-by-side as they were.

Well, not quite side-by-side. They'd had a solid wall of geese between them.

All too aware that he would feel and hear her tossing and turning as well, she'd kept herself still, nearly rigid, with her back to him and her goose brothers.

Kezzie crawled out of her bedroll, then set to work rolling it up. She nudged Ezra out of the way. "Go see what's for breakfast."

Ezra just gave her a grumpy look, fluffed his feathers, and waddled out of the shelter.

After repacking her things, Kezzie glanced around the shelter one last time to make sure she hadn't missed anything before she crawled outside, hauling her pack, bow, and quiver of arrows outside with her.

High King Alexander pushed to his feet from where he'd been sitting on a rock. The dark circles beneath his eyes showed how little he'd slept. His brown hair lay damp and tied back in the style of the Kanawhee warriors with an eagle feather fluttering near his ear. He held out a piece of jerky. "We should get moving. The Pohatomie are bound to be up early and on our trail."

Zeph, Josiah, and Ezra gathered by Kezzie's feet. Zeb wasn't in sight, so he must be flying over the forest, keeping a watch for the Pohatomie.

Kezzie stared at the piece of meat, unable to take it from him because that would communicate acceptance.

After a moment, Zeph waddled over, grabbed the jerky with his beak, then waddled back to Kezzie. She took it, chomping a bite and trying not to think about goose saliva all over her food. "Zeph, reckon we should break the shelter down so it's less obvious where we are?"

The high king eyed the shelter for a few seconds, then shook his head. "No. I doubt we'd be able to disguise our trail enough to hide that we came this way, and trying to do so would take up valuable time. We're better off hightailing it out of here."

Right. They shouldn't waste time. After the rough night, it was a relief that they wouldn't have to do the extra work of tearing apart the shelter they'd worked so hard to build.

She couldn't nod to let him know she agreed. Instead, she reached for the oilskin they'd used as a door. "In that case, you'd better come with us, Oilskin. We still need you to keep my pack waterproof."

She wrapped her pack with the oilskin, tucking it in so that everything would stay dry. With one last glance around their camp to make sure they hadn't left anything behind, she led the way down the bank to where they had stashed the canoe. After stowing her pack and weapons, she and the high king lugged the canoe into the stream.

With a glance at her, the high king climbed into the prow of the canoe again. "I have some experience steering, but you likely have more."

She'd half expected him to take the stern and the job of steering. In her experience, men usually claimed that spot for themselves rather than put the control in someone else's hands. As the high king, if there was anyone who was used to control, it would be him.

Instead, he had ceded the control to her readily enough.

As soon as she settled into the canoe, the high king put his back and arms into shoving away from the bank into the middle of the stream.

As he had before, Ezra settled onto the front of the canoe. Josiah perched on her pack in the center while Zeph took off into the air once again. After circling them once, he flew over the stream, disappearing into the sky somewhere ahead of them. Scouting ahead, most likely, while Zeb watched behind them.

They paddled in silence for several long minutes before the high king partially swiveled on his bench. "How far into the mountains does this stream go?"

Kezzie squeezed her eyes shut a moment as she pondered that. She had traveled this direction once, when her family took an extended tour of Buckhannock during some of the brief interludes of peace just before the high king was awakened.

Even though she wasn't that familiar with the territory, she could picture the map of the kingdom. As long as she was on the rivers, she could find her way around without getting lost. Her lack of knowledge would only be a problem once they had to leave the river system.

"What do you think, Josiah?" Kezzie put all her focus on her brother instead of looking at the high king. "I reckon we can take this stream and some of the side creeks nearly all the way to the border with Pohatomie if we have to. Though I hope we find Uncle Daemyn and Rosanna long before that."

Josiah stretched his neck and gave a short honk. As if he really was having a conversation with her.

"I hope so too. The last thing we want to do is get

ourselves lost while trying to find Daemyn and Rosanna." The high king faced forward again, though he tipped his head slightly toward her as he spoke.

He was handling the odd aspects of having a conversation with her rather well, answering her even as she spoke to one of her brothers. Or to the canoe. Or to a nearby rock. People so rarely took it well outside of her family.

Josiah honked again, then nudged the back of the high king's arm with his beak.

"Yes, I agree." The high king glanced over his shoulder at her goose brother, a smile quirking his mouth. "It's still strange seeing you as a goose, Josiah. For once I'm not the one dealing with a curse. It's rather refreshing to be on this side of things."

Josiah honked, then whacked the high king harder with his beak.

The high king winced, then flicked his paddle, showering Josiah with a spray of water. "Don't look at me like that. I slept for a hundred years for my curse. Though looking back on things, the curse wasn't as bad as I'd feared, at least from my perspective. I hope your curse ends up less a curse than it seems at first."

Josiah honked back, flapping his wings. In the prow of the canoe, Ezra gave something like a goose huff as he ruffled his feathers.

Kezzie gave herself over to the rhythm of paddling for several minutes as she let those words seep into her. It was strange, hearing from someone who had been through a curse and come out the other side.

Her parents and grandparents had had curses and broken them years ago. But they'd been so wrapped up in worrying over their children's curses that perhaps they'd lost a bit of the perspective that the high king had, having broken his curse more recently.

Most days, it felt like her curse would never break. Her whole life had been defined by it.

Would her curse someday feel less a curse than it seemed right now? Would she ever be able to look at it with the thankfulness she heard in the high king's voice?

That seemed impossible.

They lapsed into silence as they paddled farther north up the stream. Despite the current against them, they still made good time, the peaceful, forested banks passing by even as the sun slowly rose, warm and beaming, into the clear sky.

As noon approached, Zeb returned, circling the canoe once and honking, before he dropped between the trees. He landed on the pack in the center so heavily it caused the canoe to rock, shoving Josiah out of the way as he did so.

With something almost like a squawk, Josiah flopped from the canoe into the water.

Kezzie leaned into the rocking motion, fighting to keep the canoe steady. In the prow, the high king did the same.

After giving Zeb a hiss, Josiah flapped in an ungainly run across the water for a moment before he got into the air, his wings beating to get him above the trees. Once in the sky, he turned and headed back downstream to take over scouting.

High King Alexander glanced over his shoulder, looking at Zeb. "How far back are the Pohatomie?"

Zeb gave a honk, then tapped his beak five times against the high king's arm.

"Does that mean they're five miles back, Zeb?" Kezzie dug in her paddle, turning their canoe around a bend in the stream.

Zeb nodded, shifting until he was more thoroughly settled on the pack.

The high king faced forward again, digging his own paddle into the stream. "Five miles is something of a head start, at least, but we can't let up our pace."

Kezzie would've nodded, but her curse wouldn't let her. The only answer she could give was digging in her paddle and sending the canoe upriver as quickly as she could.

The high king must've understood, for he matched her pace. After a moment, he glanced over his shoulder at Zeb. "Thank you, Prince Zebediah, for keeping watch for so many hours. Take the time you need to rest."

Zeb held the high king's gaze for a long moment, as if assessing him. Then he tucked his head beneath his wing and fell asleep within moments.

After several more hours of paddling, Kezzie spotted a muskrat swimming through the water off to the side of the canoe.

Shipping her paddle, she slowly drew her bow and an arrow out of the oilskin covering. It wasn't easy stringing the bow while sitting in the canoe, but she managed after a moment. She lifted her bow and nocked the arrow, barely noting as the high king glanced at her. He, too, went still, letting the canoe drift. She gauged the drift, the muskrat's motion, the breeze. Then she drew, aimed, and released.

The arrow zipped through the air, then took the muskrat through the head. It twisted in the water for a few seconds before it went still.

Putting her bow aside, she took up her paddle again

and steered the canoe to the floating, dead muskrat. She fished it out by the arrow, then plopped the thing into the canoe.

As she grabbed her paddle again, she met the high king's gaze. His eyebrows were scrunched with questions that she couldn't answer directly. With both Zeb and Ezra dozing, she didn't want to address them.

That left her canoe. She tapped the canoe with a foot. "Falada, the town's only a mile or two ahead. It wouldn't do to show up empty-handed."

"No, it wouldn't." To his credit, the high king's lip didn't even curl as he sent a glance to the muskrat's wet body dumped on the bottom of the canoe. "Let's get a move on, then. I don't know about you, but I'm eager for something besides dried meat."

"It's all very well for you, Falada. You don't need to eat." Kezzie leaned into her paddlestroke. "And my brothers can fend for themselves, eating river weeds and whatever else geese eat. But I would dearly love hot food."

High King Alexander shared a smile with her, then faced forward again. They lapsed into silence as they put their backs and shoulders into the paddles, speeding the canoe upriver.

After several more twists and turns, the solid wall of trees crowding the river ended, opening to farm fields cut into a spot where the mountain flattened into a broad meadow. A few cabins tucked into the forest and around the fields while a town crowded the spot near the river, complete with a tall stockade of sharpened logs surrounding it.

The high king looked over his shoulder. "It might be best if we don't give our names. Just say you're a Rand and leave it at that. Definitely don't mention I'm the high king."

She just stared back at him. It wasn't like she was saying anything to anyone. If she so much as opened her mouth, she'd be deemed odd, at best. Or they'd suspect she was noble and under a curse.

The high king's mouth quirked into a wry expression. "Right. Best leave the talking to me. Though I'm not sure I can pull off the role of simple traveler. I've been practicing my mountain speech, but I ain't got it right just yet."

Kezzie would have winced if she could have. He didn't sound a'tall like one of the mountainfolk. The townsfolk would peg him for a castle boy from the first words out of his mouth.

But they didn't have much of a choice. While she had practiced her mountain speech, she couldn't speak to people.

She steered them toward one of the docks jutting into the stream. As the high king reached out and grabbed the dock, the old man who had been setting on a rocker under a tree nearby tipped his hat up, then stopped his rocking. He planted his feet on the ground, his hand on the nearby ax though he didn't pick it up. "Welcome, travelers. Where're you bound?"

"We're bound to the north." The high king shipped his paddle, but he didn't make a move to climb from the canoe. "Mind if we take supper in town? We got a muskrat to contribute to the tavern's pot."

Kezzie just smiled and kept her gaze just above the old man's head so it looked like she was smiling along. The high king didn't sound like he was from the mountains, but his speech had taken on a slightly rougher edge. He at least didn't sound like he was the high king.

The old man tipped his head toward the stockaded town. "Yore welcome to come on in and set a spell. Don't make no trouble, and you won't get none from us."

"Thank you kindly." Alex climbed out of the canoe, then tied the prow to the dock.

Kezzie eased onto the dock, tied the stern of the canoe so it wouldn't drift, and retrieved her muskrat. She gave Ezra and Zeb stern glances, as if they were pet geese instead of her brothers. It wasn't too uncommon for the mountainfolk to keep tamed geese for eggs or meat. Hopefully the townsfolk would think nothing of her brothers sitting patiently in the canoe for them. "Keep a wary eye on the canoe."

Her brothers blinked at her, then tucked their heads beneath their wings again. At least they had the sense not to nod and give away that they understood more than normal geese.

"Don't you fret none." The old man patted his ax, then tipped his hat over his head again. "Yore geese and canoe are safer than a mole in a hole."

The high king nodded, even though it wasn't likely the old man noticed. High King Alexander waited until she fell into step with him before he headed for the stockade.

It was only a short walk along a dirt path to the open gates of the stockade. A few of the men and women tending the fields halted and glanced up at them as they passed before returning to their work.

Inside, the town only held a minimal bustle since most of the people were presumably finishing their work out in their fields or returning home for supper at their own tables. Only those in need of something from town were out and about.

At least the tavern was easy to spot. People lingered on

the porch, enjoying a pint or telling some yarns. The sounds of laughter and music flowed from inside.

The high king stepped aside and let her go in first. A true gentleman, that one.

She pushed inside, then meandered her way through the tables. At the back, she found the countertop, where the barkeep was polishing a glass while he waited for the next customer. Unlike some taverns, this one was spick-and-span as a spring daisy, and the towel he was using was white and fresh. At their approach, the man bobbed his head to them. "Welcome to Pine Lick. What'll you have, strangers?"

Focusing on the man's towel rather than his face, she held up the muskrat, mentally presenting it to the towel.

The high king gestured to the animal. "We brought a muskrat for the pot. Will that get us a spot of supper?"

The man nodded, then reached across the bar to collect the muskrat. "I'll be back with some stew directly. My wife has a pot simmering in the back. Make yourselves comfortable."

High King Alexander took a seat at one of the tables, and Kezzie joined him. The locals sitting at the other tables eyed her and the high king, clearly discomforted by the strangers in their midst.

In a few moments, the barkeep returned with a bowl in each hand, setting one in front of each of them. "The bread will be another few minutes."

"Much obliged." The high king glanced around, then lowered his voice. "Do you have a town council or a sheriff here?"

"Yes." The barkeep crossed his arms, his brows lowering in a glower that had Kezzie's heart pounding harder. He didn't offer anything else.

The food smelled rather nice. She didn't want to get thrown out of town before they had a chance to taste it.

"We wanted to warn you. There's a band of Pohatomie on our trail. They'll be along shortly. We didn't want to bring trouble to your town, but they were going through whether we stopped here or not." High King Alexander gestured to Kezzie with his spoon. "She's one of the Rand Clan."

The barkeep's eyes widened, and his gaze swung to Kezzie. Something in his manner changed. He gave a slightly deeper nod to them. "I'll alert the townsfolk. We'll give those Pohatomie what-fer."

"Don't go causing trouble on our account." The high king kept his voice low. "We just wanted to warn you, not get your townsfolk hurt trying to take on Pohatomie warriors."

"It wouldn't be the first time we've tangled with the Pohatomie." The barkeep grinned and clenched his fists, showing off his rather impressive muscles. "We won't take 'em on long. We'll just delay 'em a mite. It'll be fun to scrap with the Pohatomie again. It has been far too quiet in these hills since the high king declared peace."

High King Alexander ducked his head, but not before Kezzie caught the flash of a smile before he stuffed it away. When he glanced up, he was solemn again. "Thank you. We would appreciate the breathing room."

The barkeep nodded. "Just enjoy your stew. Let us know if you need anything a'tall."

Kezzie blew on a spoonful of stew, then popped it in her mouth. The rich flavor coated her tongue, and she closed her eyes a moment as she savored the warmth. She hadn't bargained on this journey going so awry. She might be tougher than most princesses, but she still had missed hot food and a soft bed more than she cared to admit.

Yet she wasn't going to complain, especially since the high king hadn't complained a wit since commencing this trip, and he'd been the one sleeping without a bedroll and making do with nothing but the clothes on his back.

This had been quite the adventure. But, strangely, she wasn't regretting a moment of it.

CHAPTER 10

ALEXANDER

After they finished their stew, Alex asked the barkeep for directions to whatever served as the mercantile or trading post for the town.

As he and Princess Keziah strolled across the dirt square of the town, he caught her questioning gaze. "I reckoned we should pick up some supplies while we're here. Another bedroll and some more vittles wouldn't go amiss." And maybe a change of clothes for himself, though he wouldn't mention that out loud in front of the princess.

She didn't nod, but some of the confusion eased from her face. She must have been wondering why he was lingering when they should have hightailed it for the canoe as soon as they finished eating.

Perhaps they should have. But this opportunity to grab some supplies wasn't something he was going to pass up. He hadn't been looking forward to another night huddling beneath her cloak to stay warm.

At the trading post, all it took was mentioning that Keziah was a Rand for the proprietor to bend over backwards to help, even when Alex had to confess he had nothing to trade in return for the goods.

Perhaps the proprietor had some inkling of who they were—at least, who Princess Keziah was—for he didn't bat an eye when Alex requested pen and paper, wrote a note for King Omri, and asked if a runner could be sent to take the note to the king.

Hopefully the note would make it to the king. Something in Alex's chest eased at the thought that, once King Omri got that note, he would send Buckhannock's army into the hills to clear out the Pohatomie. He'd also send word to Alex's seneschal about King Cassius via the Rand family message system.

If the note made it. There were an awful lot of Pohatomie between the town of Pine Lick and Castle Firlin.

As soon as they finished, they hurried to the canoe. Alex untied the canoe while Princess Keziah stowed their new supplies. Besides a bedroll and change of clothes for Alex, they'd acquired more food and anything they thought could be helpful for a rescue attempt, including a coil of rope, more arrows for Keziah, and a second knife for Alex.

Sometime while they'd been in town, Zephaniah had returned, and Ezra was now gone.

As Alex climbed into the canoe, Prince Zephaniah gave him a sharp look with his beady, black goose eyes, as if he was convinced Alex had been up to no good with Princess Keziah in town.

Alex gripped the paddle, dipping it into the river once the princess had settled into the stern. "Don't look at me like that, Prince Zephaniah. We were just taking a few moments to eat hot food and fetch supplies. The town is going to slow the Pohatomie down."

Zephaniah flapped his wings, still glaring at Alex as if he still thought the trip had been a waste of valuable time.

Something about the look brought a smile. Prince Zephaniah might be a goose, but his glare was exactly like the one Luke Rand had given Alex all those years ago.

"Did you know that I met your great-great-grandfather Luke Rand over a hundred years ago?" Alex glanced from the two goose princes to Princess Keziah.

The princess met his gaze briefly, her face going strangely blank in that way he was beginning to recognize was caused by her curse, before she focused on Prince Zebediah. "I reckon Uncle Daemyn mentioned that at one point."

Alex tried not to wince. What had Daemyn told this part of his family about that trip? Alex had been at his worst back then. He'd still had so many lessons to learn, so many experiences yet to shape him. "Luke roped me into going on a buffalo hunt. I was convinced I was going to be trampled."

Zebediah gave a series of honks that were probably a laugh. Zephaniah fluffed his feathers as if he agreed with whatever Luke had put Alex through back then.

Maybe it would be best to turn to a different subject. "I was also there when your great-grandmother, the princess of Buckhannock, received her curse and her gift."

Princess Keziah's eyes widened before her gaze dropped to Zebediah. "Do you remember what Grandpa Omri said about her, Zeb? She was his mother, after all, and the one who married into the Rand Clan. She married Great-Great-Grandpa Luke's oldest son. Uncle Daemyn died the first time while they were breaking her curse and fighting off the Pohatomie."

Alex hadn't known that, either about Daemyn's first death or the fact that it was one of Luke's sons who had married into Buckhannock royalty. While he and Daemyn had talked about some of what had happened during the hundred years Alex had slept, many of the details hadn't been all that important. Their focus had been more on building the Tallahatchia of the future.

Would he ever stop feeling guilty for what Daemyn had gone through during those hundred years? Daemyn didn't seem to hold a grudge, but Alex had seen the scars. He'd heard bits and snatches of the various ways Daemyn had died. That wasn't even counting all the scars he'd gotten from wounds that hadn't killed him.

Daemyn had forgiven him, and they'd become close friends over the past few years. But that didn't stop Alex from squirming when he thought about the past.

Help me be better than I am today. It was what he asked of the Highest Prince, every time he thought about the past. He had felt his guilt. He'd been forgiven. Now he must turn to the Highest Prince in his weakness and trust in the Prince's strength to be better each day than he'd been the day before. It was only a small beginning, but a beginning, nonetheless.

Alex brought his focus back to the conversation, even as he continued his steady paddlestrokes. "Her father was greatly distressed by the curse. I'm glad to hear it was broken."

A hundred years ago, he'd barely paid attention to the poor babe who had been cursed that day. Now, he could finally feel the ache he should have back then at that father's grief. What had it been like for that girl as she grew up under her curse to fall into a sleep like death if she ate an apple?

Her curse had been broken, as his had been. Curses weren't meant to last forever, but to last only long enough for breaking them to bring glory to the Lord of All Fae and Men.

Keziah's expression dropped, her gaze focused on her brother once again. "We all hope it won't take Uncle Daemyn dying again to break any more curses. He has Rosanna now, and we're all right partial to her."

Alex froze, his paddle halting for a moment, before he could force himself back into motion. It took a few paddle-strokes before he got back into rhythm with the princess. "That's what we're here to prevent."

Daemyn deserved the chance to settle down and start that family with Rosanna.

Alex needed to solve this problem with King Cassius once and for all. For the sake of all Tallahatchia.

But also for his friend, so he could finally cease his watch over Tallahatchia and enjoy his happy ending.

ALEX LAID a branch on top of their shelter. It was nearly identical to the one from the night before, except this time they hadn't been able to find such a snug hideaway between boulders and trees. They'd had to make do with a fallen tree that was pinned a few feet off the ground, so it remained solid and fairly bug free. They'd built their lean-to against it, carpeting the space below with spruce and pine branches as before.

His stomach rumbled, and he couldn't help but long for more of that stew they'd had in Pine Lick.

He shook that thought away and focused on making their shelter as watertight as possible. He should be thankful for what they had. Due to the stop in town, he had a bedroll for the night. They had fresh bread and cheese to eat later for their cold meal. They'd had one hot meal that day already. It was more than they'd had the day before.

Keziah strode from the forest with another heap of spruce boughs in her arms. She dumped them on the ground beneath the shelter, then sat back on her heels. "Now you're a fine shelter, aren't you? The high king has quite the unexpected skill at shelter-building."

"Alex." His name burst from him. But the more Alex thought about it, the more he liked the idea. It was rather ridiculous for them to go around using titles when it was just them and her goose brothers. When Keziah glanced up at him, he added, "You can call me Alex. Or, at least, call me Alex when you talk about me to everything else. My name and title are a mite unwieldy."

"What do you think, Shelter? Should we go around calling the high king by his first name?" Keziah tilted her head, as if listening for the shelter's answer. Even after a long day of paddling, her dark brown eyes still held a sparkle. "Ah, yes, Shelter. I quite agree. If I am to call the high king Alex, then he had better call me Kezzie."

Kezzie. It suited her.

"I'd like that." Alex held her gaze, a dizzy feeling coming over him, as if he was falling into those deep, liquid brown eyes of hers.

Zephaniah honked, his beak biting Alex's calf.

"Ouch!" Alex jumped away from the goose and rubbed his leg. That hurt.

"Zeph! What has gotten into you?" Kezzie rounded on her brother, propping her hands on her hips.

Zephaniah just flapped his wings and honked again. Sitting on the pack a few feet away, Ezra fluffed his feathers and gave Alex the beady-eye. Even Josiah, who liked Alex the best, was staring at Alex in a way that threatened a bite. Only Zeb wasn't glaring at him, and that was because Zeb was scouting the Pohatomie's position one last time before full dark descended.

Alex didn't need to ask what had Kezzie's brothers all huffy. He shook himself and turned back to adjusting the boughs on the roof of the lean-to.

It had been a while since he'd felt this kind of attraction for anyone. But this wasn't the shallow flame he'd nursed for Mirabelle, before his curse. Back then, he'd only been attracted to Mirabelle's beauty, and all he could think about was wheedling another kiss. Not that she had been unwilling.

While Kezzie was beautiful, the reasons Alex found himself attracted to her had nothing to do with her loveliness. Or not only that. Her cheerfulness while living with her curse was attractive, as were the hints of her struggles that lay beneath. Her smile drew him while her strength and skills were inspiring. It had probably been inevitable that he'd find himself attracted to her after the hours they'd spent together in the last two days.

But he couldn't let this attraction grow into more than it was now. Years ago, Daemyn had all but ordered Alex to never court one of his nieces. And Daemyn was too good a friend for Alex to do anything but respect that boundary.

Besides, he wasn't sure Kezzie's brothers would react well. While he and Kezzie weren't exactly unchaperoned on this trip, surrounded by her four brothers as they were, they were the only two humans. He needed to be extra aware of keeping proper space between them.

After Alex added the last branch to the roof, he sat on the edge of the spruce branches piled on the floor of their shelter. Kezzie had spread out both of their bedrolls, along with the extra blankets they'd snagged in the town.

Tonight would be much more comfortable than the night before.

Kezzie sank into a seat beside him, though she left a foot of space between them. Still, Zephaniah plunked himself down in the gap, giving Alex a look as he did so.

As they had been building the shelter, the night had darkened around them, and only a hint of light remained on the horizon. The air had a chill as it whispered between the trees. Somewhere in the depths of the forest, a screech owl gave a haunting cry, accompanied by the singing of the treefrogs.

Kezzie dug into the pack and pulled out the loaf of bread and a wheel of cheese. She broke a chunk off both and handed them to Alex.

He leaned his elbows on his knees as he ate, trying to pretend he was regarding the forest more than he was her.

After a few minutes, Ezra waddled closer. He honked at Kezzie, his eyes fixed on the bread in her hand.

Kezzie held the bread out of Ezra's reach, shaking her finger at him. "No. No bread for you. Bread isn't good for geese."

Ezra honked and made a grab for the bread with his beak.

"I don't care if you don't want to eat weeds. You might have the brain of a human, but you have the stomach of a goose." Kezzie leaned away from Ezra, holding the bread even higher. "Besides, this is all the food the high king and I have. I won't use it up on you when you can find other food."

Ezra honked even more huffily before he swiveled around and stomped away, his webbed feet slapping on the rocky ground.

Alex stifled his laugh as he popped the last of the cheese in his mouth. The rich taste coated his tongue, a rather nice change after all the dried meat of the day before.

"How far back do you reckon the Pohatomie are now?" Alex tore off another bite of bread. "We took a bit of time at the town, and I'm not sure how much the townsfolk were able to delay them."

Kezzie's mouth tipped into a smile as she patted Zephaniah's back. "We'll know once Zeb gets back, won't we, Zeph? But I reckon the townsfolk will do a right thorough job of tussling with the Pohatomie. They've been doing it for nigh on a hundred years."

"That's reassuring. I'd hate to think the townsfolk got hurt trying to help." Alex chewed another bite of bread. It had gotten a mite dry over the course of the day, and he reached for his new canteen, filled with water from the town's well. "Hopefully this won't start another war with the Pohatomie."

"Reckon we'll go to war if the Pohatomie have touched a hair on Uncle Daemyn's head." Kezzie kept her gaze and her hand on Zephaniah's back.

Alex froze at that, mulling it over. He hadn't contemplated that angle yet. But he should have. "I wonder if that's part of King Cassius's plot. He had to get Daemyn out of the way, but if Daemyn isn't killed off, he and your family will cause King Cassius trouble. With the curse making everyone think King Cassius is me and with all the work I've put into uniting Tallahatchia, the rest of the kingdoms will turn on Buckhannock if they try to avenge Daemyn by killing King Cassius. Your whole family could get wiped out."

"Wouldn't King Cassius like that?" Kezzie grimaced and dug her fingers into Zephaniah's feathers. "Reckon we need to get to Uncle Daemyn and save him as soon as possible."

Zephaniah nodded, then honked again.

Alex couldn't understand goose, but he didn't have to understand to agree with the sentiment.

With a loud flapping of wings, Zebediah landed in their camp. He and Zephaniah exchanged a few honks before Zephaniah waddled from his spot between Alex and Kezzie. While Zephaniah perched next to Ezra, starting a conversation of honks and chattering beaks, Zebediah settled into the vacated spot.

"How far back are the Pohatomie?" Alex wasn't sure he wanted to know.

Zebediah bobbed his head eight times, then fluffed his feathers, settling deeper into the spruce boughs.

"The Pohatomie are eight miles back, but they've settled in for the night." Alex kept his gaze on Zebediah, hoping he'd translated correctly.

Zebediah bobbed his head once in a nod.

Eight miles was still a little close for comfort, but they'd gained three miles on them. The townsfolk must have done a right good job of delaying them.

Alex glanced from Zebediah to Kezzie. "We should get some rest. Ezra, Zebediah, Kezzie, the three of you have watch tonight."

Zephaniah honked and nudged Ezra with his beak.

With a huffy honk, Ezra waddled off the pack to instead perch on a rock with a better view of the stream.

"Looks like Ezra has the first watch." Kezzie glanced down at Zebediah. "I assume I have the last watch?"

Zebediah nodded and honked.

Alex mentally shook his head. Once again, the older brother was taking the worst watch. But at least they hadn't given it to Ezra. None of them wanted to risk that Ezra would fall asleep during the wee hours of the morning.

Kezzie rolled over and tucked herself into her bedroll at the far side of the shelter. As before, the remaining three goose brothers marched into the shelter and lined themselves up between Kezzie and Alex, giving him stern looks as they did so.

Suppressing his smile, Alex took off his moccasins, then wiggled into his own bedroll.

Funny how travel could make one thankful for the simple things in life. Like a roof overhead, even if it was just pine boughs. Or having an actual bedroll and blanket.

The smile dropped from his face, replaced with an ache. Yet some things never changed. No matter how much he'd changed over the years after his curse had ended, he still found himself attracted to someone he would never be allowed to love.

CHAPTER 11

DAEMYN

Daemyn scrambled up the rock staircase as quickly as he could manage. He barely had the presence of mind to avoid his various trip snares and triggers for the rock falls.

Something whizzed past his shoulder and clattered off the cliff wall. Daemyn snatched up the arrow—it might prove to be useful—and kept moving. At least this arrow wasn't sticking in him. The one transfixing his leg already hurt badly enough.

Another projectile whistled through the air, this time a rock flung from Rosanna's sling. She sent two more rocks into the air, giving Daemyn some cover as he clambered up the last few feet.

He rolled into the shelter of the cave, putting his back to the wall on the other side of the entrance.

"Daemyn! You're hurt." Rosanna flicked a glance over him, but she didn't move from her spot on the other side of the entrance opening, her loaded sling in her hand.

"I'm fine. Just a flesh wound." Daemyn strung his bow,

nocked an arrow to the string, and forced himself onto one knee. It wasn't the ideal shooting posture, but he wasn't sure he could bring himself to stand on the injured leg.

Rosanna's brow furrowed, her eyes filling with her worries before she focused on the forest below them again.

She didn't have to speak her thoughts out loud, for Daemyn shared them. Any wound wasn't good. It could get infected. At the very least, he wouldn't be as light on his feet as he had been. He'd be far less able to fend off the next Pohatomie attack. This wound could be the difference between life and death for Rosanna and their child.

A movement flickered between the trees below. The Pohatomie warriors were sneaking closer.

Daemyn aimed and released. His arrow zipped away, skidding off a tree near where he'd seen the movement. The warrior ducked back into deeper cover.

A strident, commanding voice called from below. "Daemyn Rand! You can't hold out forever!"

Colonel Beshko. Daemyn gritted his teeth both at the memories of his past death at her hands and the pain shooting through his body from his injured leg. He wasn't going to dignify her taunts with a reply.

"I have an offer for you." Colonel Beshko stepped into view at the point where the forest thinned at the base of the cliff. Her black hair glinted with the strands of gold woven through her braids. More jewels glinted along the collar of her buckskin shirt, bright against her brown skin and the dark shadows of the forest behind her.

"I don't trust any offer coming from *her*." Rosanna flexed her fingers on her sling, as if contemplating putting a rock between Colonel Beshko's eyes. After witnessing Daemyn's death, she didn't have any better feelings toward Colonel Beshko than Daemyn did. She kept her voice low enough that it wouldn't carry to Colonel Beshko below.

"I ain't about to neither." Daemyn found his own grip twitching on his bow and the second arrow he'd nocked to the string, all too aware of how thick his mountain accent was growing. "But if she's jawing, she ain't attacking."

"I know you love your wife very much." Colonel Beshko's tone was somewhere between wheedling and sneering. "Turn yourself in, and I'll spare her life."

Daemyn froze, his gaze shooting to Rosanna. What if this was the way he could save Rosanna and their unborn child?

He would die. There was no doubt about that. Colonel Beshko would kill him and make rather sure he stayed dead this time.

His heart squeezed painfully. He would never hold his child. Never see him or her grow up. Never live all those dreams he and Rosanna had been building.

But if Colonel Beshko spared Rosanna, would it be worth it?

"Daemyn Rand, don't even think about it," Rosanna hissed, her eyes flashing. "Even if Colonel Beshko kept her word—and I don't trust that she will—she never said she'd let me go. Once she figures out I'm carrying your child, you know she won't let our baby live, simply because the child is *yours*. So don't think giving yourself up will save us because it *won't*. It will just leave us without your protection."

Daemyn blew out a long sigh. Trust Rosanna to talk sense. "I reckon you're right." He raised his voice and shouted, "No deal. You ain't about to hurt Rosanna. She's the princess of Neskahana. You kill her, and Neskahana goes to war with Pohatomie, backed by the high king and the might of the rest of the kingdoms. Not even King Cassius wants that."

"The high king won't be a problem any longer." Colonel Beshko's shout held even more of a sneer, even as her lips curled. "Any day now, King Cassius will sit on the throne of the high king, and there isn't anything you or the other kings of Tallahatchia can do about it."

Daemyn met Rosanna's eyes, his heart dropping into the pit of his stomach like one of Rosanna's stones. Was this another lie? Or was Alex in trouble? What had happened while Daemyn and Rosanna had been fighting for their lives here in northern Buckhannock?

His grip tightened on his bow and arrow until the wood ached against his bones. There was nothing Daemyn could do to save Alex. Not this time. He couldn't even rescue Rosanna and his child. In his over a hundred years of life, he'd rarely felt this devastatingly helpless.

"I will give you time to think on it." Colonel Beshko backed into the shelter of the trees once again. "But you know you can't hold out for much longer. Not with that wound, and not now that we've gotten past your traps and snares. Soon we'll get into that cave, and once I do, I won't be inclined to show mercy."

Daemyn waited several more minutes before he relaxed and sagged against the stone wall once again. He set aside his bow and returned the arrow to his quiver, though he didn't unstring the weapon.

Blood drooled down his leg and pooled in his moccasin and on the stone floor of the cave. Time to actually deal with the arrow sticking through his leg.

Daemyn used his dagger to cut a strip from the end of his shirt. He packed the fabric into the wound around the arrow shaft, hissing at the rush of pain as he did so. "I'll take watch while you get a fire going and gather the supplies. Sorry I came back empty-handed. They jumped me before I could hunt down supper."

"I don't care about supper." Rosanna blinked rapidly, her words sharp, her face taut, looking one breath away from either crying or screaming in frustration.

That same churning panic filled his own chest, twisting in his stomach and burning up his throat.

Where was his family? If they didn't arrive soon, Daemyn and Rosanna would be making their last stand up here in this cave.

Daemyn had already fought far too many last stands. He wasn't ready to go down in a fight to the death for the final time.

Why had the Highest King granted him more life if he was just going to snatch it away only a few years later? Why give Daemyn a taste of dreams and all the longings for a family of his own only to tear it away in bloodshed?

Daemyn quelled those thoughts, painful as they were. Whatever happened, it would be the Highest King's will, and it would be good.

Even if it sure didn't feel good right about then.

But Daemyn couldn't sink into despair. Days ago, Rosanna had pulled him from that mire. It was his turn to do the same for her.

He reached out to her but halted short of touching her. His hands were coated with blood. "We ain't done yet, Ro."

Even as he spoke, a cry came from somewhere below, followed by shouts and more noise.

"Reckon they found one of my traps." Daemyn's grin tugged his face taut with pain and a grim satisfaction. Colonel Beshko only thought she'd gotten past his snares.

It seemed his woodcraft would get a few more warriors before all of them were dismantled.

Rosanna's shoulders sagged as some of the tension left her face. She even attempted her rather awful mountain accent. "No, we ain't done yet."

Daemyn checked that his bow and an arrow were ready to hand as he stretched his leg out in front of him, the arrow still piercing his muscle.

Rosanna retreated deeper into the cave. She quickly stoked the fire, filled their pot with water from the waterfall, and set it over the fire.

Daemyn alternated between watching her and watching the trail to the cave. She moved swiftly, despite the toll of the last few weeks. Her figure remained slim as she was not yet showing the evidence of her pregnancy.

He would fight to the death if it meant saving her and their child. But he hoped to the depth of his soul that it wouldn't come to that. He wanted so much more than to say goodbye before a bloody end.

He shook those thoughts away. He'd trusted his life to the Highest King many times before. He needed to trust Rosanna's and his child's life to the Highest King now.

The water boiled, and Rosanna took the pot off the fire. After grabbing Daemyn's pack, she carried it and the water over to him.

"Do you want me to..." She gestured at his leg, her face going ashen beneath her bronze-brown skin. In the past years, she'd learned the basics of caring for wounds from Zeke. But she didn't enjoy doing it.

"Take over watch. I can tend my leg." Daemyn met her gaze, the space between them heavy with their shared memories as he gave a lopsided smile. "It ain't the first time I done so."

"No, it ain't." Rosanna huffed before she returned to her spot on the other side of the opening. She picked up her sling once again, absently swinging it back and forth as if she found the weight and repetitive motion comforting.

Once she was on watch, Daemyn set to work. He cut his leggings away from the wound, exposing the arrow shaft sticking out each side.

Daemyn couldn't stifle the hiss of pain through his teeth as he tugged the pieces of his shirt away from the arrow.

Rosanna's gaze shot to him, the furrow returning to her brow. But she only glanced for a moment before she returned to staring out the opening at the forest below.

"The traps will make them think twice before they attack us, even though they got an arrow into me." Daemyn forced that smile to stay on his face, keeping his tone as light as he could past the pain.

Not that he or Rosanna would be able to sleep well regardless. When the enemy had been at the far end of the gully, they'd been able to risk sleeping at the same time during the day, trusting that Daemyn's traps would alert them should the enemy attempt to approach.

Now with Colonel Beshko and her warriors camped at the very base of their cave, they would need one of them to be on watch at all times.

Eventually the lack of sleep would wear on them. That was when Colonel Beshko would make her move.

Daemyn gripped the arrow shaft where it stuck out on either side of his leg. He gathered himself, bracing for the pain. Then he snapped the arrow shaft and yanked both halves of the arrow free.

Agony ripped through his leg. He hunched forward, biting back his cry of pain. He wasn't about to give

Colonel Beshko the satisfaction of hearing him scream, nor did he want to worry Rosanna.

Instead of tossing the arrow out the door, he set the pieces next to the enemy arrow he'd grabbed during his scramble up the trail. They could salvage the arrowhead.

Hopefully things wouldn't get that desperate. But in their situation, he didn't dare throw away anything.

At least they had fresh water. They had been cooking and saving whatever extra they could from the game he'd been catching in the valley. While it wouldn't last forever, they weren't in imminent danger of starving.

Daemyn poured some of the hot water into a hollow of rock, dipped a rag into the water, and sponged out both the entry and exit wounds in his calf. It hurt, but he kept at it. Dying of an infection would only be mildly more pleasant than dying at Colonel Beshko's hand a second time.

Once the wound was clean of debris, he dug out a small jug of Aunt Frennie's moonshine. Even his gritted teeth weren't enough to bite back his stifled cry as he poured the moonshine into his wound. It might as well have been fire burning through him.

"Daemyn?" Rosanna looked ready to drop her sling and go to him.

"Smarts just as much as I recollected." Daemyn gripped his knee for a long moment, hunching. When he gathered himself, he straightened again. "Worth it if it staves off infection."

Something he actually had to worry about, though neither of them voiced that out loud. Back in the hundred years that Alex slept, Daemyn had healed within hours, immune to infection and unable to stay dead.

That wasn't the case any longer. This wound would

take weeks to heal, if the Pohatomie and Tuckawassee warriors gave them that much time.

After the moonshine, stitching up the wound wasn't all that painful. Once the wound was stitched closed, Daemyn spread the injury with balm and wrapped his leg with a clean bandage from his pack.

By the time he finished, the last of the afternoon sun stretched long shadows into the depths of the valley. Not even a breeze stirred the branches. At least that would make any movement by the enemy obvious.

Daemyn washed his hands clean of all the blood. "All done." When she turned to him, he held his arms out to her.

She dropped her sling, scurried around the opening so she wasn't visible to those outside, and tucked herself against Daemyn's side.

He wrapped his arms around her, holding her close, and pressed a kiss to her temple. She was shaking as she curled against him, resting her head on his shoulder.

"We're in the hands of the Lord of All," Daemyn murmured against her hair. "Close your eyes. Remember that day you heard the trees singing."

"The day you died." Rosanna muttered the words into his shirt.

"You know that ain't the memory to dwell on." Daemyn held her closer. He'd been dead for the tree singing part of the day, but Rosanna had described it as best she could. Having been to the threshold of Beyond and heard the songs sung there, he could well imagine the wonder of the music she'd heard that day.

For a long moment, Rosanna remained tense, her eyes squeezed closed.

Then she released a long breath, relaxing. "Thanks,

Daemyn. I'd ask when you got so wise, but I already know."

Daemyn laughed softly into her hair. "Not all that wise. If I'd been the canny mountain boy I reckoned I was, we wouldn't be in this mess."

"Nothing else you could have done." Rosanna snuggled closer. "King Cassius laid his trap well."

"That he did." Daemyn rubbed her shoulder as he held her. Right now, their only hope was that King Cassius had messed up somewhere. Otherwise, this very well could be one of their last moments of peace.

Chapter 12

Keziah

K ezzie had done some paddling in her life, but nothing like this. Over the last week, she'd paddled from sunup to sundown, with only a short break at midday to cook whatever she managed to shoot along their way. If she wasn't paddling, she was either carrying Falada or the packs as they portaged over the mountain from one creek to the next one.

Even her fingers, which had been tough before, blistered from the miles. The high king's fingers too had blistered, then bled. He hadn't complained, just bandaged his hands and kept on paddling.

Not the high king. Alex. It had been a week, but she was still getting used to the familiarity. Yet something warmed inside her whenever she spoke his name to one of her brothers.

All their efforts had been worth it. They'd not only maintained their lead over the Pohatomie warriors chasing them, but they'd even gained another mile or two.

They were now deep in the northeastern Buckhannock wilderness, paddling along a creek that was so narrow that it didn't even have a name. Kezzie only had the vaguest idea of where they were, though if they needed to find their way back to the Buckhannock River, all they had to do was follow the creeks and rivers downstream.

Ezra perched in the prow of the canoe while the rest of Kezzie's brothers were somewhere in the sky, well out of sight as they scouted the mountains, either keeping watch for the Pohatomie or looking for Uncle Daemyn and Rosanna.

The tiny creek, dappled with sunlight and shadows, with its tunnel of arching trees overhead formed something of a secluded spot. With only one of her brothers present, this canoe ride was almost cozy. Not romantic, exactly. But something similar.

She shook herself, realizing she'd been staring at Alex's back. She needed to distract herself from her distraction.

"Ezra, do you think Alex would mind telling us a few of the stories of his trips with Uncle Daemyn?" Kezzie ducked under a branch.

Ezra honked, whacking a wing into Alex's arm, throwing off his paddlestroke.

She couldn't tell if Alex's flinch was from the wing or the request. He half-turned toward her, his expression a touch lopsided. "Some of the stories aren't very flattering to me. I don't suppose Daemyn has already told you those?"

Kezzie tore her gaze away from Alex's wry smile to focus on Ezra. "Uncle Daemyn would never tell stories that disparaged someone else, would he, Ezra? Zeke has told us some things, but not Uncle Daemyn."

"Of course." Alex shrugged, facing forward again and

resuming his paddling. "I almost wish Daemyn had told you his version. I'm sure he would've put me in a better light than I deserve. Still, you might as well hear everything."

Kezzie settled into the rhythm of paddling and the cadence of Alex's voice as he spoke about the Tallahatchia that was a hundred years ago, his desperation to end the curse, and his and Uncle Daemyn's trip all the way to the threshold of Beyond. He struggled to speak of the things he had seen there, but the light in his eyes, the awe in his voice, said far more than any words he could have put together.

Perhaps she should have been more horrified by his candor about the person he'd been, especially the way he'd treated Uncle Daemyn—or Jadon, as he'd been back then.

But she had traveled with Alex for a week now. She could see all the ways he'd changed. The fact that he was even here, paddling a canoe with his blistered hands and on his way to rescue Uncle Daemyn and Rosanna, provided visible proof of that.

Besides, she understood the desperation to end a curse. If she thought a journey to the threshold of Beyond would end her curse, she'd do it.

Perhaps she should. Uncle Daemyn would surely take her, once they rescued him and sorted out the stuff with King Cassius. Alex would, if she asked. If anyone could give her answers about her curse—could give her hope that this curse wouldn't last forever—then the Lord of All Fae and Men could.

What if she got all the way there and couldn't speak to the Highest King to so much as ask for help? What if she was still locked in silence—still cursed—even there? What if this curse cut her off even from the Highest King?

Kezzie shuddered and shoved away the thought. That

doubt had been her lingering nightmare all her life. She never voiced it even to her canoe. It was far too dreadful to contemplate outside of her darkest moments.

A honk from overhead ripped Kezzie from her thoughts just before Josiah swooped low, then splashed into the creek ahead of them. He flapped and honked in an uproarious manner, glancing between Kezzie and Alex as if trying to communicate something highly important.

"What did you see? Is there trouble ahead?" In the prow, Alex kept paddling, as if unwilling to lose time in talking.

Josiah matched their pace, still honking, though he shook his head *no*.

In the canoe, Ezra lifted his head and honked back, joining in the ruckus. Something sure had them riled.

"So there isn't trouble." Alex paused for a paddlestroke. "But someone is up ahead."

Josiah bobbed his head in a *yes* this time.

"Is it another town?" Kezzie didn't think so, unless it was a few scattered families who dared live this deep in the wilderness. After a week of traversing the side creeks, climbing higher and higher into the mountains, she and Alex were well away from the trade routes and main settlements of Buckhannock.

Josiah gave an emphatic shake of his head.

Who could be ahead of them? If it wasn't trouble and wasn't a town, who could it possibly be? Kezzie focused on Josiah. "Is it Zeke and Asa?"

Josiah gave a honk, then a shake of his head. He flapped his wings as if impatient it was taking them so long to guess.

Alex's eyes widened. "Did you find Daemyn and Rosanna?"

Josiah nodded so hard his whole neck moved.

Finally. Kezzie's heart pounded. "Are they all right?"

Josiah nodded, but something about his honking turned a tad more frantic. They were all right, but they were in trouble.

Alex dug his paddle in even deeper, setting a quicker pace. "Lead the way."

Josiah flapped his way back into the air, flying only a few feet over the water of the creek.

After a few more winding bends, Josiah swooped to the right, down an even smaller creek.

Kezzie turned the canoe that way. Here, the branches crowded so low that she had to duck and claw her way through. Only a few yards up the creek, her paddle scraped the bottom.

Alex fended them off a rock. "I don't reckon we'll be able to go much farther by canoe."

Likely not. The creek only grew shallower from there, gurgling over rocks and its sandy bottom.

"What do you think, Falada?" Kezzie patted the side of the canoe. "Does that stand of willows look like a likely place to turn off?"

"I don't know what Falada thinks, but I reckon it looks good to me." Alex glanced over his shoulder, grinning at her.

That grin made her stomach do funny flip-flops. No one besides her family, including Uncle Daemyn and the extended family, had ever taken to her curse the way Alex had. He treated her like it was perfectly acceptable to talk to canoes and geese and random objects instead of carrying on a conversation like a normal person.

Even more than that, he'd treated her brothers like they were themselves, geese that they currently were.

Tearing her gaze away from Alex, Kezzie turned the canoe into the slightly deeper bend beneath the willows. In the prow, Alex held the branches aside, then hopped out into the knee-high water. He held the canoe steady while she climbed out. Ezra, too, flopped off the prow, then swam toward the bank.

Together, Kezzie and Alex picked up the canoe and carried it onto the bank, finding a sheltered spot beneath the willow where the canoe would be hard to spot.

Ezra waddled up the bank, then fluffed his feathers, shaking water from their tips. Josiah continued to circle overhead, waiting for them. Zephaniah and Zebediah were still off somewhere, scouting.

Alex unlaced their packs, then shrugged into his with the ease of someone used to travel. He glanced down at Ezra. "Do you plan to fly or would you like to be carried a while?"

Ezra honked, then waddled up to Alex.

Alex knelt. "Hop on."

Ezra flapped his wings, then gave a jump, lifting high enough into the air to land awkwardly on top of Alex's pack, whacking him in the head with a wing as he did so. Ezra shifted around for a minute before he settled into a spot.

Kezzie froze, not sure what to think at the sight of the high king not only carrying his own pack, but also carrying her brother. Weren't high kings supposed to be stuffy and soft?

Then again, Alex had proven over and over again that he was neither. Perhaps he once had been. He'd told her that himself. But he was that kind of high king no longer. Now, he had a good dose of mountain to him.

Why did she find that so annoyingly attractive? She'd thought her infatuation with the high king after that brief meeting at Uncle Daemyn and Rosanna's wedding two years ago would evaporate once she spent actual time with him.

But it was getting worse—much worse. And she wasn't quite sure what to do with it. She might be a princess, but she couldn't even think about courting the high king. He was the high king, and she was cursed that she couldn't talk to people.

Oblivious to her thoughts, Alex slowly stood, waiting for Ezra to adjust his balance so the goose didn't fall off the pack with the movement.

Ezra wobbled but found a spot where he was steady. He gave a happy honk.

Alex winced. "Do you have to honk so loudly next to my ear?"

Ezra swiveled his head, placed his beak next to Alex's ear, and honked even louder.

"Wrong question. Do I have to remind you I'm the high king?"

This time, Ezra nipped Alex's ear along with the honk.

Alex sighed and rubbed his ear, though his mouth quirked with a smile. "I should have known better."

Ezra fluffed his feathers and settled more securely on top of Alex's pack.

Overhead, Josiah honked, as if impatient they were taking so long to get going.

Kezzie couldn't help but grin. They had been lollygagging. They might as well walk and talk.

Alex must have had the same thought for he set out, leading the way along the creek. Kezzie fell into the step behind him, just far enough back that she wouldn't get whacked in the face by the branches Alex pushed out of the way.

Not that she had to worry that much. Unlike her brothers, Alex was rather conscientious about carefully letting go of the branches so that they wouldn't whip backward toward her. He was less conscientious about the goose perched on his back, and Ezra got a few facefuls of leaves.

Josiah flapped overhead, leading the way. Since he could fly faster than they could hike, he would get a ways ahead of them, then circle around to get them back in sight before flying ahead once again.

Forcing a smile, she turned her attention back to Alex. Just in time to spot the leaves Alex was about to step into.

She opened her mouth to shout a warning, but her words stuck in her throat. She couldn't call out to him to warn him. She couldn't even grab him and pull him out of the way because even that would be too much communication.

Even when she turned to Ezra, she couldn't make her tongue work. Her thoughts were too much on Alex. The warning too focused on him for her to turn it to Ezra.

Tearing her gaze away from Alex, she focused on the plant, shoved past him, and knelt before it. "Naughty plant. You were about to get Alex all itchy."

Alex stumbled, catching himself on a nearby tree. Ezra honked, flapped, then tumbled from his perch on Alex's pack.

Once Alex had regained his balance, he peered over her shoulder, his shadow falling over her. "Itchy? Oh, is that poison ivy? Daemyn has been teaching me to recognize it, but I'm terrible at it."

She couldn't smile at him. She couldn't even acknowledge his thanks.

All reasons she could never be more than merely infatuated with the high king.

CHAPTER 13

DAEMYN

Daemyn stared into the fading twilight of evening, his bow in hand, an arrow nocked to the string.

Colonel Beshko would make her move tonight. He could feel it in the air and taste it on the breeze.

Rosanna rose from her spot beside him. "I should throw together some kind of stew from whatever odds and ends we have left."

Daemyn nodded, though he didn't take his eyes away from scanning the gully below.

Even if Colonel Beshko didn't attack tonight, he and Rosanna would be out of food soon.

A dark shape flapped against the hazy sky. Some kind of large bird, by the looks of it. While it was an easy target, there was no point in shooting it. It would fall into the enemy camp, and he wasn't about to provide them with a nice goose supper.

Strangely, the goose kept right on toward the opening of the cave.

Daemyn ducked out of the way as the goose soared inside and landed in a heap on the floor.

Or maybe he could get a goose for supper after all. He slowly turned, lifting his bow and arrow. Across the cave, Rosanna froze by the fire.

As if utterly oblivious to the danger, the goose waddled straight up to Daemyn, cocked its head at Daemyn's leg, then met his gaze and honked.

Daemyn had the perfect shot—almost too close—but something made him hesitate. There was something too bright, too intelligent in the goose's gaze. Almost like Rosanna's brother Berend when he transformed into a bear. Was it the same thing for this goose?

Rosanna tiptoed closer to Daemyn, whispering, "This isn't a normal goose, is it?"

"No." Daemyn's gaze remained focused on the goose, waiting to see what the goose would do now.

The goose stretched out its neck and tapped its beak against the moccasin on Daemyn's good foot. Not a steady rhythm. This was a series of quick taps, then longer spaces between the taps. Almost like...

Like the family message code. They normally used it for lights that could be seen in the mountains for miles at night. But the rhythm was the same.

I...am...Josiah.

"Josiah?" Daemyn searched the goose's face, trying to see his nephew within the goose.

The goose looked up long enough to give Daemyn a nod before he went back to tapping.

But of course Josiah was a goose. That had been his curse, which Daemyn had missed thanks to Colonel Beshko.

Daemyn's family had come. After all this time, his family had come for him after all.

Both Daemyn and Rosanna remained frozen as Josiah continued tapping out his message in the family code. Finally, Josiah stopped and gave one last honk.

Daemyn nodded, then shifted to better face Rosanna. "Alex is here. He's been traveling with Kezzie, Josiah, and their brothers."

There was so much relief in those words. King Cassius hadn't killed Alex, as Colonel Beshko had said. Alex was alive, and he was here to rescue Daemyn, of all the impossible things.

"Does he have his guards?" Rosanna fisted her fingers into her leggings.

Daemyn grimaced and shook his head. "Apparently Alex ran into some kind of trouble. While these Pohatomie and Tuckawassee kept us busy, King Cassius jumped Alex and his guards. He used some kind of cursed item to take Alex's place and tried to kill Alex. Alex escaped and joined Kezzie and her brothers."

Alex hadn't died, but from what Josiah had described, he'd sure had a rough time of it.

"And they went after us? They didn't go for help?" Rosanna glanced from Daemyn to Josiah.

Josiah ruffled his feathers and honked.

"Apparently the Pohatomie were canny, and they cut Alex and Kezzie off from help. But Alex sent a note from a local town to Castle Firlin. So the army should be clearing the Pohatomie out as best they can." Daemyn clasped Rosanna's hand, hope filling him for the first time that day. "Zeke and Asa are also on their way to find us, but they didn't have the help of geese scouting by air. Josiah doesn't know where they are at the moment."

"Hopefully they didn't run into trouble. There are an awful lot of Pohatomie and Tuckawassee skulking around Buckhannock at the moment." Rosanna reached out and rested a hand on Josiah's back. "Thank you for coming."

They had help. Alex sure wasn't the help Daemyn had been expecting, but he wasn't going to complain.

"Is there a plan?" Daemyn glanced out at the valley for a moment before turning his attention back to Josiah.

Josiah honked, then tapped at Daemyn's foot again.

"You're getting the lay of the land first." Daemyn nodded. He gestured at the valley below. "Do you have rope?"

Josiah nodded and honked.

That would make things much easier.

"If you or one of your brothers fly the rope up to the top of the cliff and secure it somehow, we can climb out of here." Daemyn pointed upward, to the roof over their head. "We'll need a distraction so the Pohatomie don't pick us off while we're climbing."

He and Rosanna would be sitting ducks, silhouetted against the cliff's face. But it was their only chance.

Josiah nodded and honked again, turning toward the opening.

"Here, let me provide cover for you." Daemyn picked up his bow and arrow again and faced the cave mouth.

Josiah took a running leap, then hurled himself out. He flapped frantically for a moment, looking caught between flight and falling.

There was movement down below, and Daemyn shot toward it. The last thing he wanted was for his enemies to kill Josiah while Josiah was trying to rescue him and Rosanna.

After another moment, Josiah's wings caught the air,

and he rose higher in the sky. Within minutes, he was high above the valley, well out of arrow range.

Rosanna returned to the fire with a lightness to her step. "I'll get to work on that stew. We'll need our strength for climbing."

"Yes, we will." Daemyn's heart beat harder at the almost painful hope coursing through him.

His family had come. Alex had come.

Perhaps he and Rosanna had a chance of surviving this after all.

CHAPTER 14

ALEXANDER

Alex lay on his stomach on the ledge, peering over the cliff at the mouth of a narrow gorge, hemmed in by tall sandstone walls and thickly forested alongside the creek flowing through it.

Down below, the fires of the Pohatomie camp formed a glow in the fading, early evening twilight. This close, Alex could see the bustle, even if he struggled to count the numbers through the dense foliage.

Kezzie lay next to him with Josiah and Ezra wedged between them. Zebediah was checking their back trail while Zephaniah flew overhead to make sure no Pohatomie scouts stumbled across them.

"I see the cliff where Daemyn and Rosanna are hiding." Alex kept his hand low as he pointed. "If we tie my dagger to the end of the rope, one of your brothers can fly it up there and wedge it securely between rocks."

Josiah tapped Kezzie's leg, then mimed limping.

"One of them is hurt?" Alex frowned. "Rosanna?"

Josiah shook his head.

"Daemyn?"

Josiah nodded.

That would complicate things. But if it was only Daemyn's leg, then surely he could still climb his way out silently enough. He'd done far more perilous sneaking in his rather long life.

Kezzie tapped Josiah. "We have a bigger problem than Uncle Daemyn's leg, Josiah. It's a clear day and looking like it will be a clear night. It will be dark, but the moon will light up Uncle Daemyn and Rosanna just about as much as daylight."

Right. He hadn't thought of that. The cave mouth was somewhat tucked away, but the top of the cliff was fully visible. Once Daemyn and Rosanna started climbing, they would be silhouetted as a moving shadow against the rock reflecting the starlight.

Kezzie might have been raised in a castle, like he was, but she was far more mountain than he would ever be, even after all this time.

"We need a distraction." Alex glanced from the two geese to Kezzie. "Any ideas? Anyone?"

Normally, Daemyn was the one who came up with the plans. Alex's plans usually led them to disaster.

This time, Daemyn had given them the bare bones. But it was up to Alex to fill in the rest of it.

Josiah gave a soft honk, and Kezzie patted his back. "I know you'd like to provide a distraction. And I'm sure four geese diving on their camp would be distracting. But you'd make too easy of a target."

"Kezzie is right." Alex took in the bustle down below. "There are far too many of them. You'd be taking too great a risk that one of you would be shot."

Worse, they had another problem none of them had voiced just yet. The longer they waited, the closer the Pohatomie warriors chasing them would get. If they didn't rescue Daemyn and Rosanna quickly and get out of there, they would find themselves pinned between two enemy war parties. Their grand rescue would end in disaster.

Sneaking was out. Head-on was out. What was left?

Something clever.

He'd been given the gift of intelligence. If ever there was a time to use it, it was now.

Staring at the camp below, he wracked his brain. But the more he thought, the more empty his mind felt.

Some intelligent high king he turned out to be. He'd come all this way, yet he couldn't even figure out how to rescue Daemyn and Rosanna. He wouldn't have made it here without Kezzie and her brothers. He'd even nearly stepped into poison ivy earlier that day.

Poison ivy. Now there was an idea.

Alex turned to Josiah. "You're a goose. You can safely pick poison ivy. Could you and your brothers pick a bunch of poison ivy and drop it on the people sleeping in the camp below? And all over their stacks of weapons? We'll wait an hour or two, then Daemyn and Rosanna can attempt sneaking up and out. If they're noticed, the poison ivy should cause enough chaos to give them cover."

Even if the poison ivy wouldn't cause a rash right away —unless one was particularly susceptible to it—no one messed around with poison ivy or wanted it on their clothes and bedrolls, knowing the rash and discomfort it would cause later on.

"They will need more of a distraction than that, won't they, Josiah?" Kezzie touched her bow. "Nettle and I will provide more cover. Alex will have to help Uncle Daemyn and Rosanna once they get down from the cliff. We can all meet at the canoe."

Alex's throat squeezed tight. "I don't like separating and leaving you."

Kezzie huffed and poked Ezra. "Alex thinks I'll be in danger. I'm the one with the four of you to protect me. He's going to be on his own. Think he'll get lost between here and the base of that ridge over there?"

She had a point. He was dismal at navigating, and they'd only gotten this far because of her and her brothers.

That still didn't make him want to leave her alone, especially not if she planned to take on the Pohatomie.

Josiah honked and whacked the back of Alex's head with his wing.

"Thanks, Josiah. Yes, we'll be fine. It isn't like we're going to fight them. Just distract them." Kezzie grinned, as if she thought it would be fun.

"We'll have to be prepared for a quick getaway." Alex shivered. The Pohatomie wouldn't be distracted by the poison ivy for long. If they woke because of Daemyn and Rosanna's escape, this could go very badly, very quickly.

"Josiah, why don't you show Alex the path to the base of the cliff? You can get the rope in place, let Uncle Daemyn know the plan, then fly back. The rest of us can start gathering the poison ivy." Kezzie nudged Ezra.

He honked in return.

Splitting up now made the most sense. Better if Alex was in place, not making noise, when it came time to move.

That didn't mean he had to like it.

Alex rested a hand on Kezzie's arm, waiting until she looked at him. "Stay safe. Don't take chances. Daemyn wouldn't want any of you risking yourselves for him."

She met his gaze, just staring back at him.

A lump filled his throat at the urge to say something profound and encouraging in this moment. It was foolish. He'd see her again before the night was over.

"You're strong. I know you'll be triumphant tonight." Alex forced a smile. "It's me I'm worried about."

Josiah honked and fluffed his feathers.

"You're right. I'll have you, Josiah. I would definitely be lost if I didn't have your help." Alex scooted back from the ledge to put the Pohatomie out of sight. He met Kezzie's gaze one last time. Wanting to tell her to stay safe. To be careful.

But he had to trust she could take care of herself. She had proven how resilient she was over their week of travel.

Instead, he just nodded, forced himself to turn away, and climbed down from their perch.

After a few moments, Josiah flapped overhead, leading the way into the forest.

Alex kept most of his attention on where he put his feet to walk as quietly as he could. He wasn't nearly as quiet as Daemyn, but he was far better than he'd been a few years ago. He no longer broke every stick in the forest.

He circled around through the forest, down by the creek where they had left the canoe. He took their rope out of the canoe and hooked it over his shoulder. The long coils weighed heavily, but he gritted his teeth and kept walking. After using some stepping stones to cross the creek, he plunged deeper into the forest.

At least it would be difficult to get lost in this part of the forest. As long as he kept the ridge to his left, he would be fine.

Josiah swooped low, then landed at the base of the cliff.

He didn't honk. This close to the Pohatomie camp, they didn't dare make noise.

Alex eased the rope from his shoulders. It should be plenty long enough to reach from the top of the cliff to the ground on this side with rope to spare. Long enough that he could risk shortening the rope by adding a few knots in it to help Daemyn and Rosanna with the climb.

After taking a few minutes to add a knot every three to four feet, Alex unbuckled his knife from his waist. He wrapped the rope around the sheath, then the hilt to make sure the knife didn't slide out. He tied the end in one of the knots he'd learned while traveling with Daemyn and tested the strength of the knot several times before he held the rope and knife out to Josiah.

Josiah lifted a foot, flexing it. With the webbing, his feet were not designed for grabbing and holding.

As if coming to the same conclusion, Josiah reached for the rope just below the knife, clamping it in his beak.

Alex held the rope with plenty of slack so that it wouldn't impede Josiah's take off.

Josiah hopped and flapped and finally got off the ground. With some effort, he weaved between the trees, working his way upward.

Alex paid out the line, preventing it from causing any tension that would tug Josiah from the air. Geese were strong, but the rope was heavy for a bird to carry.

After a few minutes of hard flapping, Josiah landed among the rocks at the top of the cliff, disappearing from Alex's sight. Within a few moments, he was back, and Alex handed him the other end of the rope to take up and over the cliff wall. Once again, Alex guided the rope until it was out of his reach so it didn't tug on Josiah or snag on trees.

When Josiah and the rope were gone, Alex found a nook in the cliffside and settled in, wrapping his cloak around himself.

Now, all there was to do was wait and hope that Kezzie's side of this escape went as smoothly.

CHAPTER 15

KEZIAH

After Zephaniah returned from scouting, Kezzie gathered Ezra, Zeb, and Zeph to help her pick poison ivy. She covered her hands all the way up to her elbows, then marched into the forest to find as much poison ivy as possible.

She'd decided to sacrifice one of her shirts, and when she found a patch of poison ivy, she laid the shirt on the ground. She grabbed handfuls of the ivy plants, yanking at the vines that trailed unexpectedly far through the forest.

Her brothers used their beaks to break off the vines, adding more and more poison ivy to the pile.

Once they had exhausted that poison ivy patch, they moved on to the next. When they had filled her shirt to bursting, she returned to the spot where she'd planned to set up, dumped out her shirt, then returned to the forest for more.

After about an hour, Josiah returned and joined them in gathering poison ivy. By the time she had a mound of it heaped among the rocks, they'd exhausted all the poison ivy in the area.

She also had a rash rising in places on her hands where the wrappings had shifted while she had been picking. What she hadn't mentioned to Alex was how prone she was to the rash. Apparently her gift of good health didn't extend to poison ivy rashes.

If it saved Uncle Daemyn and Rosanna, then the itching would be worth it.

By this point, darkness gathered in the forest, darkest in the depths of the gully, though some light remained along the western horizon. When Kezzie peeked over the ridge, the Pohatomie down below gathered around their fires, eating their supper, talking, and laughing uproariously.

Good. If she and her brothers could sneak down there, they could rub poison ivy all over their blankets before they noticed.

Grabbing a mound of poison ivy, Kezzie motioned to her brothers, then set out through the forest again.

Each of her brothers grabbed wads of poison ivy with their beaks, then flew into the air.

She tiptoed through the forest, her footsteps silent. Due to her curse, she'd spent a great deal of time hiding away with Asa and Zeke's family, learning the ways of the mountainfolk.

She kept her eyes peeled for Pohatomie guards. But it seemed they were more concerned with watching the valley than they were the forest on their other side. As far as they knew, they had Uncle Daemyn pinned with no help coming.

As she approached the camp, she slowed down, crouching. All the Pohatomie were still clustered around the fires, staring into the light and killing their night vision. As long as she moved slowly, she could easily get to their packs and bedrolls without their notice.

Easing forward at a crouch, then on her belly, Kezzie wormed her way to the first bedroll and pack laid out near the edge of the camp. She stuffed poison ivy into the bedroll, rubbing a few of the leaves all over the blanket and pillow. She wrapped the pack and extra weapons there with ivy.

One by one, she did the same to the other nearby bedrolls.

Her brothers swooped low, dropping poison ivy just outside of the fires' light. They couldn't flap their wings, which would make noise, so they had to soar as best they could until they were past the camp. Ezra nearly ran into a tree, but he managed to twist at the last moment and swerved to avoid it, even though it was ungainly. Luckily, he didn't honk.

She belly-crawled her way to the next set of bedrolls and packs, giving them the poison ivy treatment.

By the time she finished, the talk around the fires was quieting. She needed to get out of there. It was nearly full dark, the perfect time for Daemyn and Rosanna to make their move before the moon rose too high in the sky.

As she wiggled her way deeper into the cover of the forest, Kezzie scattered as much poison ivy around as she could. The whole area around the camp was now a poison ivy trap.

After another fifteen minutes of creeping through the forest, she reached the safety of the creek by the canoe. She stripped off the wrappings and washed her hands, arms, and face in the river. Before picking the poison ivy, she'd left out soap, knowing she'd want to get the oils off her hands as soon as possible.

She then washed her shirt. Since she'd sacrificed her spare shirt to carry the ivy, she didn't have anything else to change into. Hopefully this shirt wasn't too saturated with poison ivy oils. The damp buckskin stuck uncomfortably to her skin in the cooling night air.

She slathered her hands with river mud to cut down some of the itching. Once done, she made her way back to her perch in the rocks overlooking the camp. She readied her bow and checked her quiver. Shooting with her hands swelling with poison ivy rash wasn't going to be easy, but she'd have to deal with it.

She still had a pile of poison ivy left. As her brothers landed around her, she pointed at the pile. "If we need to create more of a distraction, you can drop this on their heads while I shoot. Just time your flights between my shots. I'm not sure how accurate I'll be right now."

Zephaniah eyed her, then waddled over to inspect her hands. After a moment, he speared her with another glare, as if he was angry at her for persevering even after the wrappings around her hands had shifted.

"It couldn't be helped." She gritted her teeth and tried to resist the urge to scratch. The itching was only going to get worse.

At least she wouldn't be the only one itching. Misery loved company, especially when that company was an enemy who had been trying to kill her family.

Down below, the Pohatomie slowly drifted away from the fires and climbed into their bedrolls. So far, no one seemed to have noticed anything amiss.

Kezzie squinted at the dark cliff where Uncle Daemyn and Rosanna had been hiding. Was that a darker shape against the rocks? She couldn't tell.

At least if she could barely see them—if that was them

—even when she knew where to look, then the Pohatomie likely wouldn't either.

The night grew darker, colder. But the moon was starting to peek over the treetops. In a few more minutes, the moonlight would bathe the whole area with silver.

If Uncle Daemyn and Rosanna were making their move, now was the time.

One of the Pohatomie guards leaned forward, squinting into the darkness.

He must have seen a movement by the cave. Any moment now, he'd raise the alarm.

"Time for our distraction." Kezzie raised her bow. She gritted her teeth, her fingers screaming as the bowstring bit into her rising poison ivy rash. But she drew the arrow back anyway.

She could shoot a muskrat no problem. But she couldn't bring herself to aim at the Pohatomie guards. She should. They'd kill Uncle Daemyn without a second thought.

But she had never killed anyone, and she couldn't bring herself to do it, unless they were actively trying to kill her.

Instead, she aimed at his feet, then released. This was one place her curse didn't hinder her. While she couldn't call out a warning first or threaten someone, she could shoot or stab someone as that didn't count as communication. Just violence.

The arrow zipped through the dark, then buried itself in the guard's foot. While the injury was mild, it would still slow the warrior down, preventing him from giving chase in their escape just as much as if she'd killed him.

The guard shouted in pain as he pivoted on his pinned foot, searching the rocks where she was hidden.

If he was busy looking for the mysterious archer—for

her—then he wouldn't pay attention to whatever he thought he might have seen by the cave.

The other Pohatomie and Tuckawassee warriors were waking up, rolling out of their beds. Some of them began shouting, shaking out their blankets and scratching. Utter chaos erupted as some shouted about poison ivy and others shouted about an archer.

Her four brothers took off with poison ivy gripped in their beaks. They swooped over the camp, dropping the toxic plants onto the warriors' heads.

More shouting. More chaos.

Kezzie took out another arrow. Hopefully this distraction would be enough.

Chapter 16

Daemyn

Daemyn tugged the pack onto his back, leaning his weight onto his good leg. They'd already sorted through the items, discarding anything they thought they could do without. His pack barely weighed anything at this point.

Rosanna glanced from him to the rope. "Perhaps I should carry the pack. You're wounded."

"I'm fine." There was no way he was going to make his pregnant wife carry the pack. He limped past her, then pulled the rope into the cave through the hole by the waterfall. "It's time."

The cliff by the waterfall was more sheltered from sight than if they'd climbed out by the cave's entrance. But they would still be exposed to the watching warriors.

Rosanna nodded, then took the rope from him. With a deep breath and her face set, Rosanna gripped the rope with her hands and began to climb.

Daemyn held his breath as he watched her inch upward. If she slipped, if she fell...

But it was either climb the rope or die in this cave.

Someone, either Alex or Kezzie, had tied knots in the rope, and she used them to good effect to haul herself upward. A few times, she stood on one of the knots and rested, flexing each hand in turn and catching her breath.

Daemyn perilously leaned out of the opening by the waterfall, the spray cold against his face, to watch Rosanna climb the last few feet.

Finally, she reached the top, standing on a knot for a few minutes as she tested a few of the rocks as if trying to figure out how to pull herself onto the top. After another moment, she grabbed one of the boulders and heaved herself out of sight on the top of the cliff.

Daemyn released a long breath, then reached for the rope. He gripped it with both hands and heaved himself off the ground, his body swinging out into space.

With the waterfall at his back, the spray made the rope slick, the mist dampening his clothes. He wrapped the rope around his good leg since he couldn't brace himself on the knots the way Rosanna had thanks to his injury.

Gritting his teeth, he pulled himself up hand over hand, ignoring the burn in his shoulders and the bite of the sisal fibers in his fingers.

Shouting erupted in the Pohatomie and Tuckawassee camp at the mouth of the valley, echoing off the cliffs.

Daemyn cast a glance over his shoulder. Silhouetted against the firelight, the warriors were running about, batting at themselves rather than pointing toward the cliff. Whatever distraction Alex and Kezzie had concocted, it was working.

His head reached the level of the cliff. He grabbed the same rock Rosanna had and hauled himself onto the gravelly, rock-strewn top of the promontory.

A few feet away, Rosanna crouched low next to a scrubby tree. One of the geese had wedged the dagger between the base of the tree and a slab of rock that rested at an angle.

Sticking low, Daemyn hauled the rope upwards hand over hand. Once he had it up, he dropped it over the other side of the cliff.

As much as he wanted to get Rosanna to safety first, he didn't know what or who would be waiting at the bottom. Alex or Kezzie might be down there. Or a whole party of Tuckawassee.

Daemyn gripped the rope, braced his good leg against the cliff, and lowered himself down. He had to hop-shuffle his good leg over the cliff's face, nearly losing his foot's grip several times.

He descended past the upper reaches of the trees, the utter dark closing around him. He could barely see the cliff in front of him; who knew where the forest floor lay. Inches below or hundreds of feet, he couldn't tell.

"You're nearly there." Alex's voice came from the darkness a moment before someone moved in the darkness. "I'll steady you."

Daemyn's foot slipped, and he didn't try to recover this time. As he swung upright and away from the cliff, he thumped into a body, who gave an *Oof*.

Yet as Daemyn's good leg touched the ground and he hopped to gain his balance, a strong grip grabbed his arm and steadied him.

Once Daemyn had caught his balance, he turned to the shadow standing next to him. "Thank you for the assistance, Your Highness."

Even though Alex was now *Your Majesty*, calling him

Your Highness was a long-standing, teasing joke between them.

"Glad to be of service." Alex's voice sounded tight, but the exaggerated kind of strained that showed he was teasing right back.

How far they'd come over the years, from servant and prince to friends to something closer to brothers.

The rope in Daemyn's hand wiggled, and he glanced up to find Rosanna silhouetted against the sky as she braced herself at the top of the cliff.

With two good legs, she walked down the side of the cliff with more ease than Daemyn had.

As she neared the bottom, Daemyn stepped out of her way, whispering up to her, "You're nearly at the ground."

She glanced over her shoulder, then let her feet drop. Once her moccasins were planted on the forest floor, she let go of the rope. "Daemyn?"

"Here." Daemyn touched her arm. "Alex is here too."

She propped herself under Daemyn's arm to steady him before she turned to the shadow that was Alex. "I'm so glad you're here. Things were getting desperate."

"Glad we arrived when we did." Alex motioned into the darkness. "Falada is back this way."

"Falada?" Rosanna shifted, turning in the direction Alex had indicated.

"Kezzie's canoe." Daemyn hopped to face that same direction, wincing as a stick cracked beneath his foot. He'd never be able to sneak through the forest hopping like this.

"It's going to be a tight fit." Alex tugged Daemyn's other arm over his shoulders. "We'll have to see if it even floats with four of us in it. It was designed for only one or two. We'll have to ditch most of the supplies."

Including the rope they'd left dangling down the side

of the cliff. Ditching their previous rope had led to them being trapped in that cave for two weeks. But trying to carry this rope would slow them down, and it would weigh down the canoe far too much.

As they set off into the forest, Daemyn put weight on his bad leg, attempting to take a step. Pain flared through his calf, and he gritted his teeth to stifle his groan.

But he could limp more quietly than he could hop. So he did it again, though he put more weight on Alex and Rosanna than he would have liked.

Alex directed them through the forest, circling around the point of the cliffs. It was slow going due to the darkness, the need for quiet, and Daemyn's injury.

A shout rang through the darkness ahead. Alex froze, and Daemyn swayed on his good leg before he caught his balance, using Rosanna to steady himself.

Had they been spotted? Daemyn released his grip on Rosanna's shoulders to reach for his knife.

A cluster of Pohatomie warriors held torches as they surrounded several canoes beached alongside a creek next to the small canoe Daemyn recognized as Kezzie's. The warriors weren't looking in their direction. Instead, they pointed at the end of the cliffs that overlooked the Pohatomie and Tuckawassee camp.

Alex muttered under his breath.

"How did they circle around?" Rosanna reached for the sling she'd tucked into her belt.

"They didn't." Alex spoke between gritted teeth, his tone grim. "Those are the Pohatomie that have been chasing me and Kezzie. We hoped they'd stop for the night, as they have every other night. Kezzie is up in those rocks. She's surrounded, and we're cut off from her."

Alex turned to Daemyn, as if looking at him to figure out what to do next.

Daemyn couldn't meet their gazes. What could they do now? There were now two large groups of Pohatomie and Tuckawassee warriors on this mountain. What could the three of them do against so many? Especially with Rosanna pregnant, Daemyn wounded, and Alex a high king without an heir who really shouldn't have even come after them and put himself in this kind of danger in the first place?

CHAPTER 17

KEZIAH

At the echo of voices behind her, Kezzie whirled, raising her bow and arrow. Pohatomie warriors gathered around her canoe, torches in hand, as they beached their own canoes.

Perhaps her movement alerted them. Or they had seen her pop up to take that last shot at the milling Pohatomie and Tuckawassee below. But several of the warriors behind her shouted and pointed in her direction.

Her heart pounded into her throat as her fingers shook on her bow. She was trapped. Surrounded by the enemy on both sides. There was no way she could get to the others. Nor did it matter, since their canoe was now surrounded by Pohatomie.

Kezzie drew in a deep breath, then let it out. There was nothing she could do about being trapped. She'd just have to be the best distraction possible. As long as she didn't kill any of the Pohatomie, they wouldn't get so mad that they'd want to kill her. Once they realized who she was, they would take her prisoner since she was valuable.

But once Alex defeated King Cassius, he could rescue her. She would be fine.

Her brothers honked, then took off. They swooped down at the Pohatomie, snapping with their beaks and beating with their wings.

"No!" Dropping her bow and arrow, Kezzie leapt to her feet and raced between the rocks, waving her arms. "No! Don't! Go!"

What were her brothers doing? They couldn't chase the Pohatomie off. They'd just get themselves killed.

The Pohatomie raised their weapons at her shouts, and she held her hands up, showing that she'd left her bow behind, leaving her nearly unarmed.

Zeph honked, then dove at the Pohatomie again.

"No! Go!" she all but screamed at them. They needed to get out of there. Now.

Ezra whirled, preparing to dive again. One of the Pohatomie lifted his bow and drew back an arrow.

"Ezra! Look out!" She pointed, the words burning and raw in her throat.

Ezra glanced down, then honked and flapped wildly, trying to change his trajectory as the warrior released the arrow. It zipped upward and struck Ezra's wing.

Ezra's honk was more a screech as he plummeted.

Both Zeph and Zeb swooped, catching Ezra between them. The three of them flapped and flailed, barely staying in the air.

Kezzie raced into the middle of the Pohatomie and ran full tilt into one of the warriors who was raising his bow to shoot at her brothers. The warrior stumbled, nearly dropping the arrow.

Another warrior was raising his bow, and she dodged around several warriors who were grasping at her. She hurtled into the next warrior, sending him off-balance before he could take a shot.

Josiah flapped overhead, as if not sure what to do.

She gestured to him. "Go! Get out of here!"

With a final honk, Josiah turned and soared away in the direction of the dark forest. Zeph and Zeb were ahead, with Ezra flapping and flailing between them.

Her brothers were leaving. They would be safe, at least.

As they disappeared into the darkness, Kezzie halted, then held out her hands, palm up.

The Pohatomie turned to her. Several held bows and arrows while others had daggers or swords out, all pointing at her.

"Where's the high king? He was with you." One of the Pohatomie warriors stepped forward, glaring at her.

Whatever she did, she had to buy time for Alex, Uncle Daemyn, Rosanna, and her brothers to get away.

If only she could figure out how to answer without giving away her curse. Now that her brothers were gone, there was no one she could talk to anymore. She would just have to get creative.

She kicked at the dirt. She was speaking to the earth. Not to the Pohatomie warrior. Even if he was going to be rather offended. "Well, dirt."

The Pohatomie's jaw hardened at her words, likely thinking she was referring to him. At least he was enough of a gentleman that he didn't hit her for the assumed insult.

She kept going, trying to make her voice sound high-pitched and scared. "The high king went into the valley to sneak out our friends. But he must have gotten stuck there with them. He hasn't returned."

Lying wasn't exactly the greatest thing to do, but these were the enemy. She wasn't about to point to the forest and say her friends were escaping over in that direction. And if she just kept her mouth shut, the Pohatomie would search the forest and catch her friends.

Instead, she would pretend to be a weak, helpless girl who the Pohatomie wouldn't think to question until it was too late.

She called up tears, still speaking down to the dirt. "I was trying to cause a diversion. But I must not have done a very good job."

The dirt didn't give her any sympathy.

"And the geese?"

"What do you think they were, dirt? My pets, of course. I've had them since they were goslings so they are very well trained." Kezzie gave one last kick to the dirt.

The Pohatomie swept his gaze over her, then snorted. He turned to his men. "Reinforce the others guarding the valley. We'll scout it in the morning."

Kezzie resisted the urge to breathe out a sigh of relief. Instead, she turned the sigh into a shaky, tearful hiccup.

"But just in case the high king is out here, set up a watch and scout the local area." The man turned to the rest of his men as he marched to the bank of the creek, halting next to Falada. "And just to be sure he has no means of escape..."

With a quick move, the warrior yanked his war hatchet from his belt and slammed it down into Falada's birchbark side.

Kezzie opened her mouth, but the *No* stuck in her throat.

He smashed his ax into Falada again, puncturing another hole.

"Falada!" This time, the word screamed from her throat. She lurched forward to run to her beloved canoe.

Before she got more than a few steps, Pohatomie warriors grabbed her, holding her back. She struggled, real tears blurring her vision. "Falada!"

Impervious to her cries, the Pohatomie lifted his ax again and again, smashing her beloved canoe to bits.

She sobbed, hanging from the Pohatomie's grip. Perhaps it was foolish, sobbing over a canoe.

But for years the canoe had been one of the few friends she could actually talk to. Sure, it couldn't talk back. But that had never mattered to her. She'd cherished Falada anyway.

And now Falada was nothing but bits of birch bark and fractured wood.

She barely registered as the Pohatomie dragged her away to their camp and tied her to a tree. She sagged against the ropes, ignoring the glares of the Pohatomie and Tuckawassee warriors, who had been the victims of her poison ivy campaign and now sported red spots and smeared mud.

Falada was gone. Her brothers were gone. Alex was gone.

She was alone.

CHAPTER 18

ALEXANDER

Alex's stomach roiled as he watched the geese dive at the Pohatomie warriors. Kezzie's screams reverberated in his ears and down into his bones.

"Alex, you and Rosanna head into the forest. I'll—" Daemyn pushed away from Rosanna, taking one limping step toward Kezzie and the Pohatomie.

Alex grabbed Daemyn, holding him back. "Don't even think about it. There's nothing you can do. Nothing any of us can do."

Those words were a knife to Alex's own heart. But he gripped Daemyn tightly, refusing to let go no matter how hard Daemyn struggled.

"We can't just leave her." Daemyn's eyes were slightly wild, even as his injured leg nearly crumpled beneath him.

Alex didn't like his own logic either. Everything in him wanted to race out there to help Kezzie.

But doing so would accomplish nothing. If anything, it would make her situation worse.

He gave Daemyn a slight shake, keeping his voice low

so it wouldn't carry. "There's nothing any of us can do. If you march over there, the Pohatomie will kill you. If I march over there, they'll kill me. But they have no reason to kill Kezzie. They'll take her prisoner. As long as we escape, we can rescue her later. Right now, the best way we can help Kezzie is to get as far away from here as possible. We need to make her sacrifice worth it."

Daemyn remained frozen for one more moment before he slumped and nodded.

Alex tugged Daemyn's arm over his shoulder once again. It took everything in him to turn his back to Kezzie, ignore the tearing in his chest, and set off in the opposite direction. If only he could block his ears so he didn't have to hear her shouts, then her screams.

A pained honk rang out overhead. Daemyn tugged against Alex's grip, halting as he peered around.

Alex kept his grip, but he glanced over his shoulder, trying to see through the trees. They hadn't gone far, but the trees were dense and the darkness thick enough that he couldn't see the Pohatomie or the creek. Just a glow of light and a blur of movement.

Kezzie was screaming again, though he couldn't make out the words. What were the Pohatomie doing to her? What if they were hurting her?

Daemyn, too, swayed a step backwards. It must be killing him to have to leave his niece behind like this. He'd died too many times over the years to protect his family.

Alex tightened his grip on Daemyn, shaking his head. Surely the Pohatomie wouldn't hurt Kezzie. She was a princess of Buckhannock. As long as Alex and the others got away, she would be valuable leverage both against her grandfather and against Alex.

Daemyn shook himself, then pointed to a slightly brighter patch ahead.

Alex nodded, then started forward again, taking on even more of Daemyn's weight than before.

Rosanna hurried ahead, just as the flapping of wings and a strained, low honk groaned from overhead. She reached the small clearing formed by a fallen tree just as Ezra plummeted through the canopy, an arrow through one wing. She caught him, stumbling, then falling onto her knees under his weight.

Daemyn tugged out of Alex's grip, limping forward. He touched Rosanna's shoulder, and she nodded, as if to reassure him that she was all right.

Alex knelt in front of her, taking in Ezra's wound, as the other three geese landed around them. No wonder Kezzie had been so desperate to send her brothers away. "We'll have to bind his wound quickly. The Pohatomie will start searching the forest any moment."

They had to keep moving. With both Daemyn and Ezra wounded, they wouldn't travel fast, especially on foot.

Alex eased Ezra from Rosanna's lap and into his arms instead. He'd be better able to hold Ezra still while Daemyn and Rosanna tended the wound.

Daemyn swung off his pack and held it out to Rosanna. After easing onto one knee beside Ezra and Alex, Daemyn snapped off the arrow, then eased it from Ezra's wing.

Ezra struggled in Alex's grip at the pain. Heart aching, Alex pressed Ezra tighter to his chest, holding the goose prince still. The other three geese rested their heads on Ezra's back, doing their best to be there for their brother.

When Rosanna pulled out a capped bottle of what was likely the infamous Aunt Frennie's moonshine, Alex grabbed Ezra's head and pressed his beak into his shirt to muffle any noise Ezra might make.

Good thing he did. Ezra honked and thrashed when the alcohol was poured over the wound.

Between them, Daemyn and Rosanna made quick work of padding both sides of the wing with bandages, then tying it to Ezra's body. It was the best they could do in the dark, and they'd have to examine the wound better in the daylight.

After quickly repacking the supplies, Rosanna picked up Ezra, Alex propped himself under Daemyn's arm, and they set out into the forest once again with three geese circling overhead and Kezzie's screams ringing in their ears.

As morning broke, Alex's body ached from hiking through the forest, taking as much of Daemyn's weight as he could. Daemyn had done his best to limp, but as the night lengthened, he'd leaned onto Alex more and more until he'd resorted to hopping rather than putting weight on his injured leg. As the forest around them lightened, Alex could make out the blood soaking Daemyn's bandage and moccasin.

Rosanna was panting as she hefted Ezra. Alex knew from experience that the goose wasn't light. Her arms must be aching.

Daemyn winced as he leaned his weight onto Alex to hop another step. "There's a family canoe stash in the gorge ahead. We just have to get down to it."

Alex nodded, saving his breath for taking Daemyn's weight. Getting down that gorge wouldn't be easy. He wasn't sure how he and Daemyn were going to avoid a tumble.

Zephaniah soared ahead, then swooped into the gorge ahead, disappearing from sight. A few minutes later, he flew back to them, honking and jabbing his beak back the way he'd come.

Daemyn tensed, reaching for his long knife belted at his side. "Is there trouble ahead?"

"No, that's his excited, happy honk." After over a week of traveling with the geese, Alex could tell that much, even without Kezzie's help translating. "Maybe he spotted the canoes?"

"Perhaps, though they are well hidden." The furrow remained between Daemyn's brows, his hand still on his long knife.

Rosanna hefted Ezra again, her arms shaking as she halted only a few feet from the top of the gorge. "Where is the trail down?"

Perhaps they should rest first. Rosanna was about done in, and Daemyn's face had a gray cast to it. His moccasin must be squishing with blood.

But they weren't that far from the Pohatomie. If the warriors had found their trail, they would be able to move much faster and would catch up soon.

Alex gritted his teeth. They'd have to risk the gorge and rest in the canoes. He'd paddle the canoe himself to let both Daemyn and Rosanna rest, if that was what it took.

Before he could take another step, a head appeared over the crest of the gorge.

Alex fumbled for his knife, only to remember he'd had to abandon it along with the rope at the cliff. Daemyn had his long knife half out, even as he lurched forward, as if prepared to place himself between Rosanna and danger.

Then the person took another step, pulling himself up over the crest using his grip on a tree and revealing Ezekiel Rand's dark brown hair and wide grin. "Uncle Daemyn! Rosanna!"

Alex released a long breath. As always, Daemyn's great-something nephew Zeke had excellent timing.

"We came to rescue you." Asa Rand, Zeke's older brother, appeared behind him. He stood slightly taller, his hair closer cropped.

"But I see you've already been rescued." Zeke's gaze swept over them, taking in Daemyn's leg and Ezra in Rosanna's arms. His brows scrunched. "Where's Kezzie? She set out with her brothers to stay with our family."

."How did..." Alex shook his head. Must have been the Rand family communication system. Besides, how Zeke and Asa knew what Kezzie had been up to didn't matter. Alex swallowed, unable to meet Zeke's gaze. "The Pohatomie captured her while she was creating a distraction for the rescue."

It felt like his fault, even though he had been wracking his brain to see how he could have done something differently.

Perhaps he should have encouraged her to go to her family. Maybe they could have found a way past all the Pohatomie hemming them in. Surely the Rand family could have handled a few Pohatomie following them there.

He should have been the one to take care of the distraction while she helped Daemyn and Rosanna. Sure, he couldn't shoot a bow and arrow to save his life. But he didn't have to do it well. As long as he directed a few arrows to fall within the Pohatomie camp, it wouldn't have mattered if he had been accurate.

If he and Kezzie had known how close Zeke and Asa

were, they could have waited a day to make their move. With four of them, they would have been able to pull off the rescue without getting Kezzie captured. If they hadn't been so busy with the distraction, one of the geese would have been on lookout and noticed the second group of Pohatomie coming up behind them.

So many things he should have or could have done differently.

Zeke took Alex's place holding up Daemyn. Asa glanced between Daemyn and Rosanna, as if deciding if it would be more helpful if he carried the goose or if two of them helped Daemyn.

Alex hurried forward and took Ezra from Rosanna. "Asa, help Zeke and Daemyn. I can carry Ezra."

Rosanna breathed out a sigh and rubbed her arms, as if her muscles were aching. "Thanks."

In Alex's arms, Ezra gave a mournful honk and curled his neck around to tuck his head on his back. Alex didn't know a lot about geese, but Ezra wasn't looking too good. At least the bandage over his wing wasn't spotted with blood, unlike Daemyn's leggings and moccasin.

Asa propped himself under Daemyn's other arm. With two of them supporting him, Daemyn seemed to sag further. How much blood had he lost?

Rosanna led the way down the trail, and Alex followed with Ezra. Zeke, Asa, and Daemyn worked their way down the gorge in the rear.

At the bottom, Asa directed them to the sheltered bend along the stream where they had stashed their canoe. The two of them fetched the cached canoe and placed it in the water next to theirs.

Rosanna grabbed one of the paddles, splashing to the front of the canoe. "I'll paddle for a while."

"My arms are fine." Daemyn held himself upright next to a tree, as if he knew once he sat down he wouldn't have the energy to get back up again.

Rosanna shook her head. "Tend to yourself and Ezra. You can take over once I need a rest."

"Sounds like a good plan." Zeke took Daemyn's arm again. "Let's get you into the canoe before you leave a blood trail so large the Pohatomie won't be able to miss it from a mile away."

Asa and Zeke helped Daemyn into the center of the canoe. Once he was settled, Alex set Ezra on Daemyn's lap.

As Asa and Zeke climbed into their canoe, Alex shoved the canoe into the river, then slid into it, grabbing the paddle.

His body ached. His eyes scratched with exhaustion. But he dipped the paddle into the river, putting his back and shoulders into the paddlestroke, and sending the canoe downstream, headed for Castle Firlin.

He could only hope Buckhannock remained loyal to him after he confessed that he'd gotten their princess captured by the Pohatomie.

CHAPTER 19

KEZIAH

Kezzie huddled against the tree to which she had been tied in the enemy camp, tugging her cloak around her. Her hands itched, and she clenched both her fingers and her jaw to resist the urge to scratch.

At least the Pohatomie warriors who had been chasing them had taken charge of her instead of the Pohatomie and Tuckawassee who had been guarding Uncle Daemyn and Rosanna. Those warriors were still giving her glares as they sat across the fire, scratching at their rashes.

The enemy warriors had waited for daylight, guarding the valley, before they had begun to suspect that they were guarding an empty cave. They hadn't been too happy with Kezzie after that. Especially that Colonel Beshko.

But Alex, Uncle Daemyn, Rosanna, and Kezzie's brothers had gotten away. That was all that mattered.

The leader of the Pohatomie who'd claimed her as prisoner tromped across the camp to her, then held out a piece of dried meat and a crust of bread. "Eat."

She stared, blank-faced, right back at him. Eventually, the Pohatomie warrior shrugged and set the plate of food next to her.

Once he'd walked away, she reached out her bound hands and forced her swollen, itchy fingers to move enough to take the items of food. She didn't bother to reply. After speaking when they'd captured her, she hadn't talked since. It wasn't worth the hassle. Let them think she was simply sullen or bravely stoic.

The Pohatomie didn't seem to care whether she spoke or not. She was their prisoner, and they were going to haul her to Castle Eyota regardless.

She gnawed on the food, staring into the darkening evening without really seeing.

Perhaps she should attempt an escape. But she'd be on foot with no canoe, no supplies, no weapons, and no brothers to guide her.

At this point, she might as well stay with the Pohatomie. They, at least, were feeding her, which was better than starving in the forest while on the run alone.

Not to mention, they were taking her to Castle Eyota. Sure, she didn't want to be a pawn for King Cassius, but it would be easier for her brothers to rescue her if they knew where she was. Not to mention that Castle Eyota was Alex's stronghold, even if King Cassius was currently wearing Alex's face.

Besides, she was a princess. If she could find a way to escape on her own, she would be better off doing it at a castle.

As the evening progressed to night, the Pohatomie settled down by their fires to sleep. With such a large force, they had plenty of warriors to set a thorough and alert guard patrol.

Kezzie wrapped herself in her cloak and tried to get as comfortable as possible next to the tree, missing cozy shelters, her goose brothers warm against her back, the soft sound of Alex's breathing behind her.

She curled tighter. She didn't want to cry. Again. But she was just so alone.

She'd been alone all her life in many ways. The inability to communicate had cut her off from others her whole life. Yes, she'd figured out a way around it. But it wasn't the same as being able to look someone in the eye and speak from the heart.

How could she ever get married? Could a husband live with knowing that she could never tell him she loved him? Could she raise children when she couldn't hold them close and speak soothing words to dry their tears? What kind of life would that be?

It wouldn't be fair to them. They would need more from her, and she couldn't give it because of her curse.

She'd never let herself dwell on it before. But Alex had made her think and feel things she never had before.

Worse, Alex was *High King Alexander*. Sure, she might be a princess. But she was cursed. Broken. She couldn't be the high queen. She couldn't stand in front of the court, unable to speak to the people. It would never work, even if Alex was intelligent enough to understand her strange way of communicating.

If she let herself sniffle a bit, well, could anyone blame her? She kept her crying soft enough that the Pohatomie wouldn't hear. They'd already witnessed enough of her sobs.

"Keziah."

The voice called through the darkness, tugging her from dreams of silence and running.

"Keziah."

A warm breeze whispered against her cheek, and she blinked her eyes open.

It was still night. The Pohatomie slept beneath their blankets while others strode in their patrols. Yet their movements were strangely slow, as if they slogged through a swamp.

"Keziah. Come." Her name danced on the wind again, so insistent that she found herself climbing to her feet before she'd even made the conscious decision to do so. How could she resist such a command? Such a call?

The ropes fell away as if they were blades of grass. None of the enemy warriors looked her way as she strode through the camp, following the echo of her name on the wind.

Despite the depth of night, the stars overhead glowed bright, the forest illuminated so brilliantly that the fires behind her were mere dim glows.

Kezzie crept through a forest that was just a bit more alive than normal. A song wafted on the breeze, so clear and yet just out of reach. Despite lacking a cloak, the night was warm as a hug around her and scented with something delightful and undefinable.

The breeze tugged her along, the forest growing still brighter around her, until she stepped into a clearing filled with a riot of blossoming wildflowers.

In the center of the clearing stood a man dressed in white buckskins. She'd never seen him before, yet she knew him.

He was the Highest Prince. Son of the Lord of All Fae

and Men. The one Alex and Uncle Daemyn had told her so much about. Her family had served the Highest Prince so loyally, and yet she had been filled with so many doubts. So much anger.

"Keziah. Do you know me?"

She opened her mouth, even knowing it wouldn't do any good. Knowing the words would stick in her throat, choking off as they always did. And yet...

"Yes. You are the Highest Prince. I've heard the stories about you all my life, and now I'm here before you and I..." She trailed off. She was speaking *to* him. "Why can I speak to you? My curse..."

"I am the Highest Prince, the promised Cursebreaker. No curse can stand between me and those who are mine." His eyes were so warm and understanding that she found her knees buckling, and she barely remained standing.

She pressed a hand over her mouth. She could talk to him. For the first time in her life, she could speak to another person face-to-face.

For one glorious moment, the joy bloomed both wondrous and painful in her chest.

Then the years and years of torment, of loneliness, of bitterness crashed into her, darkening the forest around her as if a cloak had wrapped around her.

When she spoke again, the words raged hot in her chest and burned across her tongue. "Why? Why me? Why do I have this curse? Why was I made to suffer like this my whole life? Why did you do this to me?"

By the time she finished her questions, she was shouting, her fists clenched at her side, the Highest Prince a blur through the angry tears filling her eyes. She panted at the force of years of bitterness pouring out of her.

"This curse, as with all curses, was given to fulfill the Highest King's purposes and for his glory."

That answer should be enough. She should be like Uncle Daemyn, her grandparents, her parents, her brothers, and the entire Rand Clan, who all trusted the Highest King and his son with such confidence.

"But why? What purpose does it serve?" Kezzie was just about begging now, her fists still clenched. "I need to know."

Despite her shouting, her anger, the Highest Prince still regarded her with that aching depth of compassion. "Keziah. Do you know me?"

"Yes, I know you." She gritted her teeth, something still boiling so fiercely in her chest that she dared speak the next words. "I'm just not sure I trust you."

As soon as that sentence left her mouth, she felt the weight of the words settle on the clearing. The breeze died. The light vanished. Even the flowers around them drooped.

For the first time, the look on the Highest Prince's face grew stern, all compassion banished from his eyes. "If you do not trust me, then you do not know me."

Those words were like a hammer blow shattering through her. She sank to the ground, curling inward.

Were there any words more awful than those? What had she done? How far she'd walked away from the trust she'd once clung to as a child.

She hugged herself, shaking under the tiniest wisp of a breeze brushing her face. No. No, she didn't want this. She didn't want this pain. This darkness. She'd had the chance to speak, and instead everything she'd spoken had been *wrong*.

The breeze strengthened, tilting her face upward with the gentleness of a parent's touch.

The Highest Prince knelt before her, already regarding her with eyes that were once more filled with warmth and compassion. "But those who know me will trust me. No curse can stand between me and those who are mine, not even this."

She shuddered beneath those words, longing for the hope found in them. She needed to trust, no matter how hard it was. The breeze strengthened around her, bolstering her. She couldn't live in this despairing darkness any longer. Not anymore.

"I know this is supposed to be for my good, and I know the curse is promised to be broken." She was sobbing now, hunched on her knees among the flowers. "But it is so hard to trust. Please help me?"

Still kneeling before her, the Highest Prince held out a hand. "I say again. No curse can stand between me and those who are mine."

With shaking fingers, she laid her hand in his. As his fingers closed around hers, she was flooded with the warmth and strength imparted by his grip.

As she released a long breath, a peace she hadn't felt since she was a child washed through her.

The Highest Prince released her hand and gestured at the clearing. "Stay. Enjoy my rest."

The words settled over her with an extra balm. "Thank you." She sank back to sit on the forest floor, digging her fingers into the soft grass.

As the Highest Prince sat across from her, she found herself talking about nothing and everything, just enjoying the kind of communion she'd never been able to share with another person.

Yet this was far better because this was fellowship with the Highest Prince of All.

She woke to cold and ropes and Pohatomie warriors surrounding her. Had last night been a dream? A hallucination?

It didn't matter. It was true, and that was enough.

CHAPTER 20

ALEXANDER

Castle Firlin rose on a hill over the river, imposing along the horizon.

Alex dug in the paddle, taking his turn in the stern of the canoe to give Rosanna a rest while Daemyn had the seat in the prow. They'd been rotating through the three of them so that one of them could rest.

Ezra rested in the center of Asa and Zeke's canoe while the other three geese were now swimming around the canoe. Zeke had a particularly energetic rhythm to his rowing now, likely anxious to get back to his pregnant wife. Or, perhaps, his wife and newborn, if she'd had the baby by now.

Alex eased the canoe closer to where Zephaniah was swimming. "I know you're all mad at me for getting Kezzie captured and having to leave her behind. I'm mad at myself. But if you'd like to have it out with me, I'd rather we got it out now before I get yelled at again by your parents and grandfather."

Zephaniah gave him that beady-eyed stare he'd been

giving him the whole trip back from northern Buckhannock. He lashed out and gave Alex a hard bite on the arm.

Alex flinched, but he didn't break his paddling rhythm. "I deserve that."

Daemyn glanced over his shoulder. "Zeph, I thought we had decided there was nothing more Alex or any of you could have done. If Alex is to blame, then so are you. And so am I."

Zephaniah gave a honk and flapped. Was that agreement with Daemyn? Or more argument?

Alex wasn't sure he wanted to know.

As the castle loomed high on the mountain overhead, Alex directed the canoe to the castle dock, following in Zeke and Asa's wake. Well, time to get yelled at again.

"You got my granddaughter caught by the Pohatomie, my grandson shot, and now you come here begging for warriors to take back your crown? Again?" King Omri of Buckhannock sat on his throne, his gaze firm, his voice biting, despite being over eighty years old.

Alex resisted the urge to flinch. Put that way, why would the king of Buckhannock help him anymore?

He was a pathetic excuse for a high king. Sure, he'd rebuilt Tallahatchia's economy. He'd organized the rebuilding of the bridges, encouraged the trade routes.

And yet every time he turned around, someone else was trying to take his crown or curse him or both.

Did he even want to take his throne back? It was far more trouble than it seemed to be worth. Perhaps he should just let King Cassius have it and be done with the whole mess. King Cassius might be a conniving, power-hungry man, but he was, by all that Alex had observed, a good king. Pohatomie was flourishing.

Except that King Cassius had Kezzie, and Alex couldn't leave her there.

Daemyn and Rosanna stood at Alex's side with Zeke and Asa on the other side of them. For once, Daemyn's family connection wouldn't help Alex. Daemyn, too, was feeling guilty over getting cornered and needing rescue, leading to Kezzie's capture and Ezra's injury. This time, he would not speak up and use his pull as King Omri's great-uncle.

Strangely, Zephaniah, Zebediah, Josiah, and even Ezra waddled to Alex's side and clustered around him. As if lending him their support.

Alex drew himself straighter. He would have to be the high king and speak for himself.

"I know I'm culpable in your granddaughter's capture. I won't deny that." Alex held King Omri's gaze without looking away. "But Princess Keziah is strong. The decision to rescue Daemyn and Rosanna was as much hers as mine. She made the decision to cause the distraction, and she knowingly surrendered to buy us the time to get away. I will not disrespect her strength by saying I should have overridden her decisions to keep her safe."

King Omri glared for another long moment before he sighed and nodded. "She is a Rand, yet she has always felt she had more to prove because of her curse."

"It is likely the Pohatomie are taking her to Castle Eyota so that King Cassius can use her as further leverage." Alex gestured in the direction he guessed was south. "All I'm asking is for an escort so that I can return to Castle Eyota safely. The Pohatomie have trespassed on Buckhannock's sovereignty by sending their armies into your countryside. Even beyond King Cassius's impersonation of me, this is a disrespect of Buckhannock that must be dealt with, and as the high king, I will deal with it."

King Omri nodded. Then he, finally, stood and gave Alex the deep bow that he should have given his high king when Alex first arrived.

But Alex didn't hold the slight against him. He understood. He'd messed up by getting Kezzie captured and Ezra hurt. He blamed himself.

But, in the end, King Cassius was the one to blame for all of it. He had invaded Buckhannock. Tried to kill Daemyn and Rosanna. Tried to kill Alex. Captured Kezzie. He'd use Kezzie as bait or leverage if he had the chance.

King Cassius had a lot to answer for. And as the high king, Alex was going to make sure he answered for all of it.

ALEX STRODE through their camp deep in the mountains between Buckhannock and Kanawhee, occasionally stopping to check with the Buckhannock warriors.

Accompanied by the squad, their trip had been uneventful and free of Pohatomie since leaving Castle Firlin.

With so many warriors present, there was nothing for Alex to do. The dishes were done. Bedrolls laid out. Shelters built. It was strange, stepping back into the role of a high king who could just sit back and do nothing while others set up camp.

Well, he hadn't exactly done nothing. He had created his own pallet of spruce boughs and spread out his own bedroll. No reason for someone else to do that much for him.

Alex strolled across the camp, then lowered himself to the ground next to Daemyn.

Daemyn sat with his back to a rock, his bad leg stretched out in front of him. Rosanna was already asleep in the shelter a few feet away, her back to them.

As much as Alex needed every ally he could get, Zeke had stayed behind to be with Isi, who might have the baby any day now. Asa, too, had stayed behind to be with his brother and sister-in-law.

Even with all that, Daemyn and Rosanna had chosen to come with Alex, even though he'd given them the option of staying behind as well. That was not a loyalty he would ever take for granted.

Alex gestured to Daemyn's wound. "How's the leg holding up?"

The injury had healed somewhat during their canoe ride to Castle Firlin. But now they had to hike over the mountains, and they were sticking to a tough pace to reach Castle Eyota as quickly as possible.

At least the bandage was no longer stained with blood. Daemyn must have changed it since they set up camp.

"I'm fine." Daemyn spoke more to the ground than he was to Alex.

Alex nudged him with an elbow. "Come now. I know you too well to swallow that lie."

Daemyn gave a huff of a laugh as he leaned his head against the rock behind him. "Never thought I'd miss when you were obliviously pretentious, Your Highness."

"That's what happens when you become friends instead of just prince and very put-upon manservant." Alex shifted to find a more comfortable position against the rock. There was a sharp point digging into his back. "So. The truth."

"I've had worse." Daemyn still wasn't looking at him, hedging as he still was. But at least there was a hint of a lopsided smile.

"You've also died nine times, so that ain't saying much." Alex attempted to add a hint of mountain to his speech, knowing his attempt would be terrible.

Daemyn's smile grew, as Alex had known it would. "I ain't about to keel over from a little arrow wound to the leg. The sooner we get to Castle Eyota, the sooner we can rescue Kezzie. I ain't about to slow everyone down on account of my leg."

"Still, you got to be in good enough shape to rescue Kezzie when we get there." Alex let his head sag against the rock behind them. "And I wouldn't mind if you were there to stand with me against King Cassius. It seems I'm always needing you to rescue me."

"This time you did a mite of rescuing yourself." Daemyn gestured at his leg. "Rosanna and I were in a spot of trouble."

"Kezzie and her brothers did most of the work." Alex squeezed his eyes shut, wishing he could banish the sound of Kezzie's screams from his memory. It had been the right thing to do, but leaving her behind still killed something inside him. "And she's the one who paid the price for it."

Both of them lapsed into silence for a long moment. What was there to say, knowing Kezzie was somewhere out there, captured by the Pohatomie? Had they already arrived at Castle Eyota? Since the Pohatomie likely had gone straight there, they would arrive first.

After several minutes, Daemyn released a breath, his voice more lighthearted again. "It sounds like you and Kezzie got rather...close while traveling together. Sharing a canoe and a shelter..."

Alex held up his hands. He'd known he'd have to answer to Kezzie's family for their travels. He'd been thankful to get away from Castle Firlin without having to confess that part of the story to Kezzie's parents. "I was a perfect gentleman, promise. And it wasn't like we were alone. I was under the watchful eye of her four brothers who were more than ready to put their hard beaks to use if they thought I was crossing any lines."

Daemyn laughed and shook his head. "I ain't questioning you, Your Highness. I reckon you ain't been nothing less than honorable toward Kezzie."

"Oh. Right." Alex should've known, but he had panicked there, for a moment. Even at his worst, he hadn't pushed those kind of boundaries, yet he also hadn't always been the most honorable person either.

"Reckon it was just as well you were there." Daemyn shrugged and shifted his bad leg slightly. It had to be aching, after the long day of hiking up and over mountains. "I hate to think of Kezzie all alone as she tried to avoid the war parties of Pohatomie scouring the hills. She might have ended up captured regardless, and we might not even have known the Pohatomie had her until they revealed their hand."

That was something. It didn't ease all the guilt, but it helped.

Alex sighed and rested his arm on his knee, his other leg stretched out. "And don't worry. I know your nieces are off-limits."

As painful as that was, whenever he thought about Kezzie. But he would respect the boundaries Daemyn had laid out long ago, even if it meant breaking his own heart.

"Off-limits? What are you talking about?" Daemyn

lifted his head, his brow scrunched as he searched Alex's face.

Perhaps Alex shouldn't have brought this up. His face burned as he searched for the words to explain. "You know. Even if I was attracted to Kezzie—and I'm not saying I am —I wouldn't pursue it. You said you wouldn't want to inflict your family with me."

"When did I say that?" Daemyn glanced upward, as if searching his memory.

"Right after I woke up. That first night, on the wall top." Alex couldn't bring himself to look at Daemyn. "And it's all right. I understand. I—"

Daemyn's hand rested warm and heavy on Alex's shoulder, giving him a slight shake. "Alex." No nickname. No teasing. Not even his real title.

Alex dragged his gaze up to meet Daemyn's.

"You ain't the same person you were when you woke. I ain't neither. We've both come a long way since then." Daemyn held his gaze, his dark brown eyes filled with something Alex couldn't read. "You're a good man, Alex. If there's something between you and Kezzie, I ain't about to stand in your way."

Really? Alex let those words settle into his chest. All that time, traveling with Kezzie, he'd told himself he couldn't let himself actually fall for her. Even before that when they'd first met at Daemyn and Rosanna's wedding, Alex hadn't dared pursue that spark of attraction he'd felt.

What Alex had thought was a barrier didn't exist. If— when—they rescued Kezzie, he didn't have to hold back.

Alex managed a quirk of a smile. "Good to know I don't have to worry about your disapproval. Kezzie's four brothers are bad enough."

"They won't be as much of a problem as you might

reckon." Daemyn gave Alex's shoulder one last shake before he dropped his hand. "They would've made much more of a ruckus back in Castle Firlin if they disapproved."

What had Alex done to gain their approval? He'd gotten their sister captured. She wouldn't have even been in that situation if he hadn't talked her into helping with Daemyn's rescue.

"Also good to know." Alex settled back against the rock, peace and hope filling his chest in a way he hadn't even known he was lacking.

Now they just had to rescue Kezzie from King Cassius's clutches as soon as possible.

CHAPTER 21

KEZIAH

Kezzie craned her neck as their canoes drifted around the bend in the Kanawhee River. Castle Eyota perched high on the cliffs above, its stones slightly pink, its turrets spearing the sky. Something in her stirred at the sight of the great castle of Tallahatchia, the seat of the high kings for generations.

She'd never thought she'd travel this far and see Castle Eyota for herself. While she'd traveled between the ancestral Rand home in the mountains and Castle Firlin, the only time she'd left Buckhannock was to travel to Neskahana for Uncle Daemyn's wedding. Other than that, she'd always believed her curse would keep her trapped in Buckhannock her whole life.

Yet here she was with the city of Eyota sprawling along the riverbank and the majestic castle casting a shadow on the water before her. Too bad she was seeing it as a captive of Pohatomie warriors with King Cassius instead of Alex sitting on the throne.

The Pohatomie and Tuckawassee warriors pulled their

canoes up to the castle docks, as if they had every right to be there.

Kezzie climbed from the center of the canoe where she'd been ordered to sit. Her still rash-covered hands currently weren't bound, probably for appearance's sake. But there wasn't much point in trying to escape now. There were too many warriors around her, and Colonel Beshko would be more than happy to order her shot if she tried anything.

She didn't resist as the Pohatomie fell in around her and marched up the trail from the docks to the main gates of the castle. The band of Pohatomie and Tuckawassee led by Colonel Beshko fell into place behind them, still sporting red welts, though some had begun healing during their travels.

Guards patrolled the wall top, dressed in the colors of Kanawhee and the high king.

Even if she could shout to them, they were under the impression that Alex was the one who had returned and was currently in residence as high king. They wouldn't believe her if she tried to tell them the truth.

The Pohatomie leader gave some story about kindly escorting her so that she wouldn't be attacked by the same bandits who had attacked the high king. The guards bought it and let them inside.

The Pohatomie marched her through the gates, across the courtyard, and into the castle's keep with barely a pause.

As they stepped into the throne room, Kezzie took in the man sitting on the throne at the far end, and her breath caught in her throat.

Alex. He was giving her a warm smile, his brown eyes taking her in with such a gladness to see her that she nearly pulled away from the Pohatomie to run to him. He was here and she was safe and...

She squeezed her eyes shut and tried to take long, slow breaths of the cold draft brushing her face. When she halted, the Pohatomie pushed her forward, but she didn't open her eyes.

That Alex on the throne wasn't real. It was an illusion from a curse. Her mind knew that, even if her eyes didn't. She couldn't let herself be fooled.

The Pohatomie gripping her arm halted her.

"Welcome to Castle Eyota, Princess Keziah. I hope your travels were pleasant."

Alex's voice, but it had an edge, a slickness that Alex's real voice lacked.

Kezzie opened her eyes and glared at the person on the throne. For a moment, he still wore Alex's face. But the longer she stared, the more she told her head and her heart that what she was seeing wasn't real, the illusion peeled away until only King Cassius's blond hair and angular, smirking face remained before her.

Kezzie lifted her chin as she faced him. Perhaps it was her time in the dream communing with the Highest Prince, but King Cassius's sneer didn't shake her as much as she thought it would.

She turned her gaze to the large, wooden throne he was sitting on. "Throne of the high king, I'm sure the true High King Alexander will appreciate King Cassius keeping his spot warm for him."

King Cassius's smirk twisted even more. "It will do you no good to tell anyone the truth. Even now, you can see they will not truly hear what you are trying to say."

Kezzie glanced around. Everyone in the throne room, even the Pohatomie guards who had come in with her, had a slightly glazed look to their eyes. This was the cursed handkerchief at work, convincing them they were seeing High King Alexander.

Yet there seemed to be another, sinister layer to the curse. The handkerchief didn't just give King Cassius Alex's face, but it also induced some kind of mindless loyalty to him. After all, the Pohatomie and Tuckawassee around her hated the real Alex. Yet they were bowing reverently before the fake high king on the throne, even Colonel Beshko.

And she could still feel it, working on her. Whispering in her heart that this was Alex. King Cassius's face blurred, trying to turn back into Alex's.

He wasn't Alex, and she wasn't going to let some handkerchief tell her otherwise.

"Ah, I see, Throne. King Cassius is not keeping you warm. He's keeping you ice cold." Kezzie dropped her gaze back to the throne. Looking at it was better than looking at the smudgy curse-faced King Cassius.

King Cassius gave a derisive snort, apparently unimpressed by her show of bravado. "As you're a princess, I won't have you thrown into the dungeon. I believe a room in the highest tower would be the appropriate place to host you."

He motioned to some of the Kanawhee guards standing by, barking out orders to them.

At least she wasn't going to find herself in some hole. She'd heard from Josiah what King Cassius had done to Uncle Daemyn at Castle Fonthaven. Not that Uncle Daemyn had told her that story himself. He'd been rather close-lipped about the experience.

But a tower would be rather difficult to escape. There

would be only one stairway up, and that was sure to be packed with guards.

Kezzie spun on her heel, marching for the door and forcing the designated guards to hurry to catch up.

Once they were out of the throne room, the guards' eyes cleared. But the memories of what they believed they had seen must have stayed with them for one grabbed her arm and led her through the winding passageways of Castle Eyota. Compared to her square and simple home of Castle Firlin, Castle Eyota was sprawling with many interconnected rooms and spired towers rising toward the sky.

Eventually, they reached one of the towers and climbed flight after flight of spiral stairs until her calves ached and she was dizzy from climbing in circles.

Finally, they reached the room at the very top, and the guards shoved her inside. The door shut behind her, the lock sliding into place.

Kezzie glanced around, taking in the sparse room. The ceiling was peaked from the underside of the wooden roof while windows ringed four of the six sides. Kezzie crossed to one of the windows. It was dusty, but the pane cranked open. While it was narrow, she thought she could wiggle through, given enough motivation.

The only thing in the room was a straw pallet with a sheet and a blanket on it. Not nearly enough fabric for her to construct a rope to climb out.

At least for now, she was stuck. Nothing she could do but wait for an opportunity to escape or help in a rescue.

CHAPTER 22

DAEMYN

Daemyn leaned heavily on the wooden cane, exaggerating the stiffness in his bad leg. The blanket wrapped around his stomach beneath his shirt gave him a paunch. With his cloak pulled around him and his hair powdered gray, he looked like an elderly man stumping his way into Eyota with his just-as-elderly wife at his side.

The braids Rosanna had wrapped around her head had also been powdered with ash while she hunched beneath the ratty shawl she'd bought off a woman in the last small town they'd passed through before reaching Eyota. With her blanket padding her middle, she looked like a pleasantly plump elderly lady.

His heart warmed at the sight of her looking old and gray. The Highest King willing, Daemyn would see her like that years from now, still at his side after living a long and full life together.

He shook himself. Now wasn't the time to be

distracted. He forced his gaze back to scanning the streets around them as they trundled deeper into Eyota.

The morning bustle of Eyota closed around them, though most people were polite enough to avoid jostling what they thought was an elderly couple. Traders from Guyangahela with packs on their backs mingled with back-woodsmen from Buckhannock as they tugged along trained elk or buffalo laden with packs. Mountainmen from Monongadotte with branching antlers attached to their headdresses nearly knocked into peddlers from Neskahana with their carts laden with pottery.

At least King Cassius hadn't managed to change that much in the weeks he had been residing in Castle Eyota.

Out of the corner of his eye, Daemyn caught sight of the four warriors from Buckhannock, dressed in dirty buckskins without any distinguishing markings. Each of them held a goose flung over their backs as if they were returning from a successful hunt. The geese were doing a good job of playing dead. Josiah, especially, was flopping around limply and really selling the part.

Behind them, another Buckhannock warrior hauled a rickety handcart they'd piled with cut wood. Alex was buried under all that wood, probably enduring a rather uncomfortable ride as the cart bumped over the rutted road.

The war party from Buckhannock hadn't been too happy to send only four guards along with their princes, especially with their princess already captured, and Daemyn couldn't blame them. He wasn't too happy about Alex entering Eyota without much of a guard escort. But too many warriors descending on the town would draw too much notice.

As it was, Pohatomie guards lurked at the street

corners, searching the crowd with sharp eyes, even sharper long knives buckled at their sides.

Daemyn limped another step, pretending to lean on both his cane and Rosanna's arm, as he turned down a street leading toward Old Eyota, the first part of the town to be rebuilt upon the crumbling remains of the Eyota from a hundred years ago.

As they entered Old Eyota, the streets narrowed, the homes and shops clustered closer to the street. While nearly all the buildings were new, there was a sense of "oldness" to the place, from the old wood cladding the new homes to the ironwork that had been salvaged out of the ruins and now restored to its former glory.

Daemyn kept his head down, holding his breath that he and Rosanna wouldn't be recognized as they tottered around another corner. He lost sight of the four guards with his goose nephews and the guard with the high-king-laden cart. They were all taking different streets to get to their destination.

Partway up another, even tinier street of homes, Daemyn and Rosanna halted on the front step of a home that looked nearly identical to those around it, except for the slightly haphazard look to some of the shingles on the roof.

With one more glance around to make sure they weren't observed by any of the wandering guards, he knocked on the door.

A middle-aged woman opened the door a crack, her face harshly blank. "What is it?"

"For the true Tallahatchia," Daemyn whispered.

The woman nodded and stepped aside, opening the door wide. "Hurry up."

Daemyn placed a hand on Rosanna's lower back as she

inched her way inside. Despite the woman's urging to hurry, Daemyn kept up his appearance of shakily limping inside.

As soon as Daemyn crossed the threshold, the woman swung the door shut and put the locking bar in place. Only then did she turn to them, her eyes widening as she got a good look at their faces. She curtsied, the harsh lines fading into a warm smile. "Princess Rosanna, Daemyn Rand. It's an honor."

Daemyn gave her a nod as he leaned his cane against the wall by the door.

"Thank you for providing a refuge for us and for the High King's Council." Rosanna smiled as she took off her shawl. "Four Buckhannock warriors will be coming by shortly with the princes of Buckhannock, who are currently geese, as will another Buckhannock warrior with a cartload of wood hiding High King Alexander himself."

"The high king?" The woman's smile dropped once more as her face paled. "He shouldn't be here in Eyota! It ain't safe!"

No, it wasn't safe, and if there was any other way, Daemyn would have done his best to keep Alex far away from Eyota.

But as long as King Cassius was squatting on the high king's throne, Daemyn, Rosanna, their unborn child, Alex, and all of Daemyn's family in Tallahatchia were in danger. Not to mention, Alex was the high king the Lord of All had placed on the throne of Tallahatchia. Daemyn would stand at Alex's side through whatever it took for Alex to take his crown back.

"King Cassius is sitting on his throne, and the high king has to be here to reclaim it." Rosanna gave the woman another of her princess smiles. "Thank you once again for your loyalty. Where are—"

Berend, Rosanna's brother, poked his head out the hole in the ceiling to the loft. "Come on up, Ro-Row. You'll *bear*ly fit, but we'll make room."

And...the bear puns had begun. Daemyn resisted the urge to sigh. The bear puns were Rosanna's family thing, thanks to Berend's curse to change into a bear each night. He had recently broken that curse, but now he could change into a bear at will, so that only made him even more obnoxious when he wanted to be.

"Bere-Bear, I see you escaped the castle safely." Rosanna headed for the ladder, and Daemyn followed at her heels.

He waited for her to scramble up first before he climbed after her, rolling onto the floor of the loft at the top.

In the space made smaller by the sharp angles of the roof, Berend, Princess Ranielle of Tuckawassee, Prince Tyrell of Monongadotte, and the representatives from Kanawhee and Guyangahela sat on pallets along two sides of the loft. Only Pohatomie didn't have a representative there.

"Speak for yourself! It has been un*bear*ably boring here." Berend patted the open spot beside him and Ranielle. "Though I hear you're the ones who've had a *bear* of a time."

Daemyn shook his head. Acting as Neskahana's representative on the Council hadn't matured Berend as much as hoped.

Rosanna sank onto the open spot on the pallet. "I ain't going to lie; it didn't look good for a while there. But we did our best to *bear* the strain."

There wasn't room for Daemyn next to her, so he lowered himself to the floor in the corner beside her, stretching out his bad leg.

Berend opened his mouth, sucking in a breath as if to make another comment. But Ranielle poked him. "You can continue your conversation later, Bere. Right now, we need to get down to business." Ranielle leaned forward to smile around Berend at Rosanna and Daemyn. "As glad as I am to see both of you alive, Rosanna, Daemyn."

Across the room, Prince Tyrell gave a cough. His antler crown hung from a peg near the ceiling to keep it out of the way in the tight space. "Yes, quite. But—"

Before he could continue, another knock rang on the door. Everyone in the room fell silent, their faces going tense.

Daemyn dropped a hand to the knife he'd hidden beneath his cloak. Was that someone expected? Or a Pohatomie warrior checking out something suspicious?

Voices filtered up from below for a moment before the door clunked shut again. A honk sounded below a moment before a pair of hands shoved a goose up through the hole to the loft. The Buckhannock warrior spoke from somewhere beneath Josiah. "Could someone please take His Highness?"

Daemyn started to push to his feet, but Berend popped up more quickly, probably due to his lack of wounds.

Berend took Josiah, holding him with the goose's head facing him. "His Highness?"

"My nephew, Prince Josiah. All of the princes of Buckhannock are currently geese." Daemyn couldn't help the slight quirk to his smile. "You know how that goes."

"Oh, good to see you again, Josiah." Berend set him down to the side, then reached for the next goose being thrust through the hole. "Geese, huh? I reckon I'd rather be a bear. So much more fierce than a bird."

Josiah flapped his wings and bit Berend's arm.

"Ow!" Berend fumbled Zeb, nearly dropping him.

Zeb honked and scrambled out of Berend's grip, landing in a heap on the floor. As soon as he got his webbed feet under him, he cuffed the back of Berend's head with a wing, hissing at him.

"I get it, I get it. Geese are plenty fierce." Berend rubbed his arm, then reached for the next goose, who happened to be Zephaniah.

Zeph glared at Berend the whole time, waddling out of Berend's grip as soon as he could.

As the warrior hefted Ezra through the hole, another knock rattled the door. For a moment, everyone froze yet again. Then the warrior all but tossed Ezra onto the floor of the loft. Ezra honked, his wings splaying. His honk turned shrill. The movement must have tweaked his injured wing.

Berend grabbed Ezra, pinching his beak closed to stifle his noise.

Daemyn braced himself against the wall. As he'd learned a moment ago, he wasn't as sprightly as he usually was. If he needed to defend Rosanna, he'd better be ready.

Yet after the door closed, the voices murmuring below didn't sound concerned. The scuff of hands and moccasins sounded on the ladder a moment before Alex's head appeared through the hole, followed by the rest of him as he hauled himself inside.

"Your Majesty!" Prince Tyrell leapt to his feet, then bowed.

Ranielle, too, pushed to her feet before she curtsied.

The others clambered to their feet, but the representative of Kanawhee both bent in a bow and reached for his knife, as if he wasn't sure what to do.

The representative from Guyangahela eyed Alex. "No offense, if you are the real high king. But how do we know you are the high king? The real one?"

"It is a good question, and I wouldn't trust those in this room if you weren't willing to ask it." Alex nodded to the man, holding his hands out at his sides as he half-turned to face Daemyn, meeting his gaze. "Daemyn will vouch for me. Of everyone here, I always trust him to see through whatever curse that might or might not be surrounding me."

Daemyn held Alex's gaze, all the curses they'd seen and broken over the years weighing between them.

Instead of answering right away, Daemyn took in Alex's appearance. He was dressed in the same travel-stained buckskins he'd worn when climbing into the cart from the trip into Eyota. Slivers of wood and sawdust clung to him.

More than that, Daemyn didn't sense the shivery wrongness of a curse twanging in his soul.

He could have vouched for Alex then and there, but the others wouldn't have the assurance of knowing exactly what he'd seen that had him so convinced.

Daemyn held Alex's open, genuine gaze. "What is one thing the Highest King told you on the threshold of Beyond? That is something King Cassius doesn't know."

"That he had given me no curse. That what I called a curse would not be removed. That all things were from him." Alex's voice lowered as he spoke, rough with memories too glorious for either of them to fully put into words even all these years later.

Daemyn swallowed back his own memories of that day before he gave a nod. "He's the real high king."

The representative from Guyangahela gave a sigh and sank into a bow. "In that case, it's a pleasure to see you returned—for real—to Eyota, Your Majesty."

The others bowed as well before they all settled back into their seats. The geese settled in around Rosanna and Daemyn, with Ezra tucking in on the pallet between Rosanna and Berend. Someone found a cushion for Alex, and he took a seat at the head of the room.

Daemyn settled more comfortably against the wall and clasped Rosanna's hand in his, sharing a look with her. Whatever came next, they would survive as they always did. By sticking together and trusting in the Highest King to see them through it.

Alex tilted his head to Daemyn, meeting his gaze again. "Ready to plan a way out of yet another curse-related scrape that I've gotten us into?"

"I reckon so." Daemyn shook his head, his smile wry. "Just please make this the last time. I'm getting too old for this."

Alex grinned back, though his grin dropped from his face as he turned to the rest of the room once again. With his back straight, his head high, and a regal confidence draped over his shoulders, he looked every inch the high king Daemyn had always known he could be as he asked, "Now, what havoc has the usurping Cassius been causing in my absence?"

CHAPTER 23

ALEXANDER

As the sun set into the western mountains, Alex tugged the hood of the ragged cloak over his head, gripped his staff, and waded into the gaggle of honking, squawking geese. Four of the geese were Kezzie's brothers; the rest were the castle's geese.

The geese darted about, and Alex wouldn't have been able to keep them on the path headed for the castle gates without the added help of Zeph, Zeb, Josiah, and Ezra. The four of them headed off the other geese, honking and nipping at them to keep them in line. As a goose boy, Alex was rather ineffectual.

He didn't look around. Daemyn, Rosanna, Berend, and Ranielle were somewhere behind him, mingling with the bustle of those headed into Castle Eyota for the night. In the forest just outside of the gates, the Buckhannock warriors moved closer, though they remained in hiding.

Would all of his allies get past the guards at the gate? It was anyone's guess what kind of orders King Cassius had given the guards. There was every likelihood that Alex would be recognized and hauled in front of King Cassius as an impostor.

Which wouldn't be the worst thing, as long as there was enough of an audience.

Alex kept his head down, shrouded in the cloak he'd borrowed from the real goose boy. He hunched and tried to appear as small as possible.

The guards barely gave him a glance before waving him and the geese through the gates.

Well, getting past the guards wouldn't be much of a problem. Daemyn had been right about servants being invisible, especially if it was a servant the guards expected to see.

Alex resisted the urge to breathe a sigh of relief as he used his staff to nudge the geese toward the back section of the castle where the animals were housed.

Good thing he actually knew where that was now. Before he'd slept for a hundred years, he wouldn't have known where to start. Or how to pretend to be a goose boy.

He skirted around the stables, guided the geese past the kitchen gardens, and finally herded the geese, except for Kezzie's brothers, into the pen next to the chicken coop. Once he'd shut the gate, he turned to them. "Go find Kezzie. That's the tower she should be in." He pointed upward at the tallest tower.

Zephaniah nodded, meeting Alex's gaze for a moment. Then he honked to his brothers, and the four of them gave a short, flapping run before they took off into the sky. Ezra's flapping wasn't as graceful as the others, but his wing had healed enough that he could fly again.

Once they were gone, Alex hung the goose boy's cloak on a peg and leaned the staff against the wall in the open-sided shed to one side of the goose pen where hay and a pitchfork were stored.

After a glance around, Alex took off the ratty buckskins he wore to reveal the clean buckskin leggings and a cotton shirt in the same light blue as the castle servants' uniform that he'd worn underneath. He patted his left thigh where a sheath sewn into the buckskin hid a knife he'd been given at Castle Firlin.

With his hair down instead of tied back and the eagle feather no longer tied by his ear, Alex meandered his way to the kitchen back door. He kept his head down, trying to pretend he was invisible the way Daemyn had taught him.

Once he was in the kitchen, he grabbed one of the trays and joined the bustle headed toward the great hall where King Cassius was dining with the court right now. Alex held the tray on his shoulder like the other servants, using the cluster of large pitchers on it to hide his face.

A few of the servants gave him a second glance, but most seemed to shrug it off. With all the new servants coming and going with the visiting nobles and King Cassius's entourage, no one cared if an extra hand pitched in to serve supper.

Alex had seen Daemyn do just this so many times, but it was a strangely powerful feeling pulling it off himself.

Though it was disheartening that the servants didn't immediately recognize him as their high king, even if he was doing his best to hide. Once he'd regained his throne, he would have to do better at getting to know the servants so that they would know him in return.

He followed the parade of servants through the back passageways of the castle. The cacophony of noise that was a large gathering of talking, eating people echoed down the corridor a few moments before he turned the corner and stepped through the door into the Great Hall.

The upper windows beamed the fading, evening sunlight onto the tables of nobles, merchants, guards, and anyone else King Cassius had invited to eat at his table tonight. The room was quite full, due to the addition of King Cassius's Pohatomie and Tuckawassee warriors filling most of the tables. King Cassius would have plenty of warriors to stand at his side.

Captain Taum, Alex's seneschal, and the castle's Kanawhee guards clustered beside one of the tables near the middle. How many of them were taken in by the curse and how many of them had managed to resist? Alex wouldn't know until he set his plan in motion.

At the far end, King Cassius sat on the dais on the throne-like chair, a table set before him.

There was no sign of Kezzie, which was a good thing. If she'd been here, King Cassius would have used her as a pawn or a human shield. As long as she remained locked in the tower, her brothers could rescue her.

For a moment, even Alex's gaze blurred, and he found himself looking at his own doppelganger, the crown of the high king resting on the brow of a stately king with...

A cold draft brushed the back of Alex's neck, and he shook himself. He of all people should not be fooled by the curse. He knew King Cassius wasn't the high king because *he* was the true high king.

Alex blinked again, and there was King Cassius, sprawled on the throne and sneering down on those gathered in the Great Hall.

Alex's skin crawled. That was *his* throne. Not because he wanted the power or authority that came with being the high king. At least, not the way King Cassius desired it.

But because Alex loved these seven kingdoms with an ache deep in his soul, and he wasn't about to let King Cassius send the kingdoms back to the darkness in which they had wallowed for a hundred years.

The Highest King had given Tallahatchia to Alex to love and serve. He wasn't going to abdicate that duty to King Cassius without a fight.

King Cassius didn't understand that love or that duty. He just saw the throne the way Alex had a hundred years ago. As a source of power. A way to make himself great.

The throne of the high king wasn't about making the one who sat upon it great. It was about pouring himself out for the people and being an example of the Highest King.

Alex didn't do that perfectly. But at least he was striving for that goal, in the strength of the Highest Prince.

With a deep breath of that bracing draft, Alex set out down the center aisle between the tables, still carrying the tray. A few of the nobles motioned to him as he passed, requesting the drinks he had on the tray. Alex dodged around their hands, ignoring them.

Perhaps there was a better way to go about confronting King Cassius than marching up to him in the middle of his well-guarded hall.

But if Alex had come with a large number of warriors at his back, those warriors might have been taken by the curse too. Instead of more allies, Alex would have instead brought Cassius more minions.

The representative from Kanawhee had suggested a quiet assassination. Alex had dismissed that idea right off. Besides the fact that the assassin was just as likely to be taken by the curse before he could kill King Cassius—unless Alex asked Daemyn to do the deed, and he'd never ask that of him—Alex wasn't about to become the type of high king who ordered assassinations. This was a curse, and the only way to face a curse was to bring it into the light, not skulk about in more darkness.

That left only this one option left. Face King Cassius with only the allies he could trust not to succumb to the curse at his back and trust in the Highest King for the victory.

Walking between the tables, Alex resisted the urge to look around and search for Daemyn. There wasn't any need to do so. Daemyn would be where he said he'd be.

As Alex neared the base of the dais, he finally set the tray on the end of the table, knocking into a few of the plates and glasses. The nobles around protested, and one shouted an insult.

Alex made note of that particular noble. Perhaps he'd have to act as a peasant more often so he knew who to give a set down to for haranguing the servants.

Alex strode to the base of the dais, raised his head, and met King Cassius's gaze. "King Cassius. I am High King Alexander, and I have come to reclaim my throne."

He'd pitched his voice at the right tone to carry over the noise. The benefit to having lots of practice at doing just that.

Behind Alex, the noise faded as people stopped talking, paused eating, and paid attention to the unfolding drama.

What would they see when they looked? Two high kings? Did Cassius look like Alex and Alex look like Cassius? Or was Alex just a blur and didn't look like any particular person?

It didn't matter. The only way to confront a deceptive curse was with the truth.

King Cassius gestured to Alex. "Guards, seize him! He's an impostor attempting to take my throne!"

"I'm the true high king. He's the impostor." Alex half-turned to face the crowd, though he pointed over his shoulder at King Cassius. "He has a curse making him appear to be me. But you can see beneath it if you resist it."

For a moment, the Kanawhee warriors at the middle table remained where they were, as if torn.

Captain Taum and the seneschal rose, strode to the front of the hall, and knelt before Alex. Captain Taum spoke with something almost like anguish in his voice. "Your Majesty. I'm sorry I did not see through this curse sooner. We have been waiting for your return."

"Arrest the captain and the seneschal! They are colluding with the impostor!" King Cassius gestured to all three of them.

The Pohatomie and Tuckawassee warriors leapt forward, drawing their weapons.

Most of the Kanawhee warriors staggered to their feet and faced them. The rest looked between the two groups, still too befuddled by the curse to know what to do.

Several of the Pohatomie raced past the others and grabbed Alex's arms.

Captain Taum drew his long knife, but Alex motioned to him. "Stand down. I thank you for your loyalty, but there are too many for you to fight."

Captain Taum hesitated for a moment, even as more Pohatomie and Tuckawassee warriors surrounded them. The Kanawhee warriors paused as well, hands on their weapons. While everyone was poised to move, fighting didn't yet break out.

Alex tried not to look at the Kanawhee warriors too closely. Several of them seemed to be edging toward the dais, and if one of them was Daemyn, Alex didn't want to give him away.

King Cassius settled into a more relaxed pose on the throne. He gestured from Alex to the rest of the room. "My gathered nobles, can we let this kind of treason stand? Do we want a return to the darkness of war we have endured?"

A murmur swept the room. If anyone hadn't been paying attention, they were now.

Alex didn't fight against the grip of those holding him, but he swept his gaze over the room. "I'm not the impostor. I am the high king. I walked these halls over a hundred years ago before the curse. I saw the Tallahatchia that was and the Tallahatchia that is now. I have gone to the very threshold of Beyond. I will not bow before the curse that King Cassius would bring to these halls."

A few of the gathered people blinked. Were they seeing the truth?

"Grand claims from an impostor." King Cassius snorted, his tone sneering. The curse must be working overtime to make people think Cassius was Alex. Gesturing grandly, Cassius asked the crowd, "What do you think the appropriate punishment should be for the treason of pretending to be the high king?"

"Hanging!"

"Beheading!"

Alex refused to flinch at the shouted suggestions, telling himself that it wouldn't come to that. They'd stop Cassius long before Alex was in danger of execution.

One of the Kanawhee warriors lunged up the dais, reaching for King Cassius.

Cassius waved, and more Tuckawassee warriors charged out of the shadows behind the throne, including

Colonel Beshko. The warriors grabbed Daemyn, hauling him back before he'd gotten anywhere close to King Cassius and that cursed handkerchief.

Alex swallowed, fighting against the hold on his arms for the first time. He could speak all he wanted, but not everyone would hear. Not until King Cassius was separated from that handkerchief and the curse was broken.

King Cassius lowered his voice so it wouldn't carry. "I was worried when you got away at first. But I knew you'd come to me and solve my problems, with your loyal dog nipping at your heels. Good thing I have a few loyal dogs of my own."

Daemyn bared his teeth, lunging against Colonel Beshko and the warriors restraining him. "You won't get away with this."

"I already have. The power I carry is too strong, even for you." King Cassius smirked and tapped the front of his shirt, where he must have the handkerchief stashed. He lounged even more confidently on the throne. "However, I can't allow either of you to live."

Alex swallowed, a weight in the pit of his stomach. He didn't like the gleam in King Cassius's eyes.

"What would be the appropriate punishment for traitors?" King Cassius stroked his chin before he raised his voice again. "Impersonating the high king is a crime that must be punished so severely that no one will think to do so ever again. I declare that you and your accomplice will be placed in barrels filled with nails, then rolled down the mountainside again and again until dead. Guards, begin preparing the barrels. The execution will be carried out immediately."

Alex's head lightened, chills sweeping through him, at

the pronouncement. He'd known King Cassius hated him and Daemyn, but to decree such a death…

How could no one see that King Cassius was an impostor? Surely they knew that Alex—the real high king—would never make such a proclamation? Nor would Alex ever condemn someone to death without a proper trial.

Yet when Alex glanced around, many in the hall were wearing that glazed look. Even some of the Kanawhee warriors had loosened their grip on their weapons, and a few knives clattered to the floor. Captain Taum and Alex's seneschal glowered, but they were too surrounded by enemies to do anything but die uselessly if they fought back.

They were alone. No allies who weren't captured or fallen to the curse.

At least Kezzie would be all right. Alex had to believe her brothers would get her out and keep her safe.

Even if Alex was about to die a horrific death.

Chapter 24

Keziah

Kezzie lay on her pallet, staring at the ceiling. She'd propped all the windows open, letting in the mountain breezes. The faint sound of voices occasionally wafted through the windows from the courtyard below.

She'd sat by the window and watched the bustle for most of the day. It was the most entertainment she had in here.

How long would it take for someone to come for her? She'd toyed with ideas for escape, obviously, but she'd been forced to come to the conclusion that there was nothing she could do until someone else set a rescue attempt in motion.

Kezzie sighed and plucked at the sheet. "Too bad I can't fly. That would have been convenient."

With the flapping of wings and a honk, a goose popped through the window and tumbled to the floor in a blur of brown and black feathers.

Kezzie pushed all the way upright. "Zeph?"

Her brother honked and waddled to her as he looked around, taking in everything of her tiny room.

Rescue. She gaped at her brother, almost unable to believe it. She scrambled to her feet. "Do you have a plan to get me out? The walls are too sheer for me to climb, and the base of the tower is packed with Pohatomie warriors."

Zeph inspected her pallet, then he grabbed the corner of the sheet with his beak and tugged.

"The sheet and the blanket aren't nearly long enough to make a rope, otherwise I would have done so by now." Kezzie extracted the sheet from the bed anyway. She wasn't sure why she had such a defensive note to her voice.

Perhaps it was that niggling feeling that, as a Rand, she should have been able to rescue herself long before now.

Zeph dropped the sheet, waddled back to the window, and hopped onto the sill. He tossed himself out.

Kezzie lurched forward, leaning out the window.

Zeph fell for several yards before he could get his wings working enough to carry him aloft. He joined her other brothers soaring in front of the tower. Even Ezra was there, though he really shouldn't be flying on that injured wing. Zeph honked at the other three, then he swooped past the window, honking at her.

"What do you want me to do? Jump out holding the sheet? It won't be enough to slow me." Kezzie leaned farther out the window. It was such a long way down. She didn't relish just jumping out with nothing but a sheet to stop her fall. She'd break her neck for sure.

Zeph circled around, then honked again, jabbing his head at her as if she should know what he was trying to tell her.

She understood his frustration. She'd been there far too often, trying to communicate past her curse.

"You want this?" She held up the sheet he'd had her grab.

Another nod as he was circling around.

She held the sheet out the window. This time, it was Zeb who swooped closer, grabbing a corner. Josiah, Ezra, and Zeph all grabbed corners so that the four of them held the sheet aloft between them.

Oh, now she could see what they were up to. Kezzie shook her head. "I'm still too heavy, even for the four of you. You won't be able to hold me up."

Zeph honked around a mouthful of sheet as the four of them tried to fly in formation and maneuver the sheet below the window.

Perhaps they wouldn't be able to hold her up, but they might be strong enough to slow her fall so that she could land without being hurt.

It was either trust her brothers or stay locked in this tower.

Kezzie boosted herself up, then dangled her legs over the windowsill. Her head grew light looking down at the drop below her with nothing but her grip on the windowsill keeping her from slipping off.

One of the rocks of the tower broke off in her hand, and she stifled a scream as she nearly slipped.

Her brothers swept toward her. They couldn't hover, but they slowed as much as they could as they flew beneath her.

It was now or never. Kezzie drew in a deep breath and slid from the ledge, dropping.

Her feet landed on the sheet, and she toppled into it. Her weight yanked her brothers closer together until their wings were hitting. The sheet closed around her, and she tumbled, nearly smacking herself in the head with the rock she was still gripping in her hand. She found herself on her back, lumped in the sheet like a bundle of laundry.

Were they dropping too fast? She couldn't tell. She couldn't see. Everything was just sheet and wind and the hard beating of her brothers' wings.

She worked her legs beneath her, doing it slowly so that she didn't unbalance her brothers. She poked her head up, the wind making her eyes tear up.

Her brothers didn't seem to be dropping as quickly as she'd feared. They were falling, but the four of them were straining, holding up her weight.

"Where's Alex? Is he here? Is he confronting King Cassius?" Kezzie peered over the edge of the sheet, trying to see the ground.

Zeph gave a honk that might have been a confirmation, but it was hard to tell his tone through his mouthful of sheet.

"We need to help him." She had this bad feeling in the pit of her stomach that had nothing to do with falling from a tower with nothing but a sheet and four geese to hold her up.

Alex needed help. She couldn't have said how she knew, but she had to get to him.

Based on the position of the sun low on the horizon, it was suppertime. If Castle Eyota was like Castle Firlin, then King Cassius would be holding his court's supper, and that was where Alex would choose to confront him.

She pointed. "Head for the Great Hall. We can go through one of the upper windows."

Zeph gave a honk that sounded frustrated, but he and Zeb veered toward the Great Hall.

"I have a rock. I'll throw it through the window before we go through." If they just went through the glass themselves, they'd get all cut up. They might still get a few cuts, depending on how much the glass shattered with the rock.

Zeph honked. As they approached the Great Hall, he turned them parallel to the windows, though they were still slightly above.

Kezzie couldn't see anything inside through the glare. She threw the rock as hard as she could at the window at the end, the one that would most likely be over the dais, if there was a dais like in her grandfather's castle.

The rock flew through the air, then smashed into the window. Glass shattered before falling in a sheet of sparkling shards.

Zeph circled them around, then all four of her brothers made a beeline for the empty space. Teeth of glass rimmed the edges, sharp and glinting in the evening sunlight.

Kezzie ducked back down and tucked herself into a ball, holding her breath. If her brothers timed their entrance wrong or if her weight dragged them down more than they expected...

One of them could get hurt. Really, really hurt.

The hard flapping of her brothers' wings paused for a heartbeat, and they dropped in a stomach-lurching manner as they passed from light into shadow. Something sharp scraped against Kezzie's leg, and she gritted her teeth rather than cry out at the pain.

Then they were through, and her brothers' wings flapped again. But they were still tumbling, falling faster than they had been, as her brothers couldn't seem to get their wings to bear them up any longer.

Kezzie screamed as they fell faster and faster. Her back hit the ground, then she rolled in a tangle of limbs and bedsheet. Her brothers honked and tumbled around her, wings and long necks and hard beaks slapping into her.

As she skidded to a stop, she tore at the sheet and scrambled free of it.

At the base of the dais, Alex and Daemyn struggled against a cluster of Pohatomie and Tuckawassee guards. Near them, a knot of Kanawhee warriors fought even more of the Pohatomie and Tuckawassee. Yet more enemy warriors turned toward her.

The nobles and servants by the tables were dashing about, screaming and shouting in the aftermath of her grand entrance.

But none of them mattered. King Cassius stood before the throne, wearing a crown that no doubt didn't belong to him. The small table that had been before him was knocked over with food splattered all over the dais and the steps.

Perhaps the curse tried to work on her. But she was too angry at King Cassius, too scared for Alex, and she barely felt its slippery grasp.

Kezzie pointed at the false high king. "Get him."

Her four brothers honked, then lunged at King Cassius. He gave a squawk of his own as he fell under the weight of four geese attacking him. The crown of the high king fell from his head and rolled a few feet away.

Kezzie shoved past the table and pounced on King Cassius as well. He was flailing, trying to fend off the geese. One of his fists struck her jaw with a glancing blow, and she nearly tumbled back again.

Then Josiah stuck his head beneath King Cassius's shirt, fished around for a moment while King Cassius batted at him, and withdrew with the handkerchief in his beak.

King Cassius lunged for it, but Zeph and Zeb blocked

him with hard pecks to his face. He covered his eyes, shouting in pain as he scrambled backward.

Kezzie scrabbled on hands and knees, putting distance between herself and King Cassius, before she took the handkerchief from Josiah.

The handkerchief felt strangely heavy in her hands, the spots of Alex's blood dark and brown against the otherwise white fabric.

She gripped the handkerchief and tried to rip it. But nothing happened.

"Arrest her!" King Cassius howled, still thrashing on the floor while her four brothers attacked him.

The warriors froze, glancing between him and Kezzie. Now that she was holding the handkerchief, did she look like Alex?

The nobles and others in the Great Hall turned toward her as well. So many eyes, staring at her. Something in her quailed, and her skin itched with the need to curl up and hide.

The guards fighting with Alex and Daemyn halted, though they didn't release their grips on her friends.

Alex met her gaze, tipping his head in a slight nod.

Speak. She needed to speak.

Her legs shook as she stood before so many people. They would think her odd, speaking to furniture and objects instead of people. Just the strange little princess from Buckhannock.

With honks and hisses, her four brothers backed away from King Cassius and gathered at her feet. Only now could she see streaks of blood on their feathers. They must have cut themselves on the glass or while fighting King Cassius. Yet despite their injuries, they were standing with her.

Kezzie squeezed her eyes shut, trying to remember the peace she'd felt when fellowshipping with the Highest Prince. It had seemed like such a small thing to speak when she had been with him.

It didn't feel so small now. But she had to do it anyway.

With a deep breath that tasted of that dream forest, she focused on the handkerchief in front of her. "Handkerchief, you know the truth of the blood staining you. You are the cause of this deception. But now is the time for truth. You have made King Cassius appear to be High King Alexander. You might be making me appear to be the high king. But I am not the high king. There stands the real High King Alexander, and I refuse to appear as anything but the truth of myself."

A shiver went through the handkerchief. Gripping the fabric again in both hands, she tugged. Hard.

This time, the handkerchief ripped with a loud tearing sound that reverberated through the Great Hall with more force than it should for such a tiny piece of fabric. Just to be safe, she tore each of the pieces in half a second time.

She dropped the pieces of the handkerchief, and they fluttered down, the pieces landing on her brothers.

They craned their necks around, gripped the pieces, and tore at them, as if to make sure the handkerchief was thoroughly destroyed.

Another of those indefinable shivers prickled along her spine, though this was accompanied by a swirl of light carried on a forest breeze.

Then her four human brothers stood around her, dressed in what they had been wearing the night they'd turned into geese, though their clothes were more ripped and bloodstained than they had been all those weeks ago.

Zeb grimaced and spat out the shreds of the handkerchief. "That don't taste good."

Ezra clawed at his tongue with one hand, his other arm tucked close to his body. "Ick. That was in my mouth."

Josiah flapped his arms and heaved a sigh. "I really liked flying."

Kezzie opened her mouth to speak, her body swaying forward with the urge to hug her brothers.

But the words stuck in her throat even as her arms froze, her curse no longer letting her express herself through a hug.

Was it possible to ache through such happiness? She had her brothers back...but she couldn't talk to them.

Zeph tensed, reaching for the knife that was once again belted at his waist now that he was human. "Stay sharp. This ain't over."

All around the room, the glazed look drained from people's eyes. The Pohatomie and Tuckawassee warriors had halted, though they still had their weapons in their hands as they faced the outnumbered Kanawhee guards. The enemies restraining Alex and Uncle Daemyn hadn't let go, and Colonel Beshko seemed to be debating whether she could slit Daemyn's throat before he could fend her off.

"No!" King Cassius clambered to his feet. Bloody welts rose on his hands and face from her brothers. "Attack! This is our chance, Pohatomie! Tuckawassee! If we want to throw off the tyranny of the high king, we need to seize our freedom now!"

Kezzie's gaze shot to Alex, holding his eyes for just a moment before she was shoved backward.

CHAPTER 25

ALEXANDER

"Now!" Alex drew the knife from the hidden sheath along his thigh and sliced at one of the Pohatomie holding him. Catching the man by surprise, he managed to score a line across the warrior's abdomen. The Pohatomie stumbled back, releasing Alex.

Daemyn, too, drew his hidden knife. He barely got it up in time to block Colonel Beshko's stab at his heart. The two of them whirled into a furious knife fight that Alex couldn't follow.

The doors to the Great Hall crashed open even as a roar reverberated through the room.

A black bear charged inside, Princess Ranielle riding on his back and wielding a spear. The Buckhannock warriors raced inside after them, weapons raised.

Several of the Pohatomie warriors took one look at the enraged black bear, dropped their weapons, and ran.

Alex tore himself free from the second warrior holding him and dashed up the steps to the dais. He placed himself so that he could keep a wary eye on King Cassius while he faced the crowd.

To one side, Kezzie's brother Ezra stood in front of Kezzie, protecting her, while Josiah, Zeb, and Zeph threw themselves into the fray.

If Kezzie could find the courage to speak, then so could Alex. It was time to claim his throne once and for all.

Alex raised his voice so that it would carry, even over the fighting. "Pohatomie, your king is finished! He has committed treason against the high king and trespassed on the sovereignty of Buckhannock. Choose now whether you will stand with the high king or fall with King Cassius."

The fighting slowed as the beleaguered Pohatomie warriors glanced between Alex and King Cassius, as if trying to decide where their loyalty lay.

The Kanawhee and Buckhannock warriors had surrounded the enemy. At their head, Prince Berend huffed and snarled while on his back, Princess Ranielle brandished her spear.

Some of the Pohatomie warriors fell to their knees before Alex, either loyal to him or simply deciding which way the wind blew.

The rest of the warriors edged toward their king. Alex recognized many of them as the ones who had taken part in the ambush. They would have known about the deception all along. There was no point to them pretending loyalty to the high king now.

King Cassius's gaze darted about, as if searching for a way out.

"King Cassius, you might as well surrender now. You are surrounded and outnumbered. This entire hall knows what you've done." Alex crossed the few steps to reach his throne. With deliberate confidence, Alex sank onto it.

"And what will my punishment be?" King Cassius flexed his fingers on the hilt of his knife.

"If I were a man like you, I would say that you have already named the punishment for impersonating the high king." Alex resisted the urge to smirk at the white look to King Cassius's face.

Perhaps it was petty, but he wanted Cassius to squirm after proclaiming such an awful judgment. Cassius would have gone through with it, if Kezzie hadn't shown up with her brothers to get the handkerchief.

"But I am not like you." Alex held King Cassius's gaze. "You will be given a trial before the King's Council in full accordance with the laws and decrees of Tallahatchia. However, you know your crimes. You know the penalty for them. I will not grant you a pardon from them."

In other words, if—when—King Cassius was found guilty of both trespassing on Buckhannock and impersonating the high king, he would be executed according to the law. Alex would not grant King Cassius the mercy of a pardon.

Maybe it was harsh, but King Cassius had proven time and again that he was out for power. He had no true remorse for the things he'd done. He would have killed Daemyn, killed Alex, and kept Kezzie as a pawn to use against her parents.

While mercy was part of Alex's duty as the high king, so was justice.

King Cassius's gaze burned. With one move, he raised his knife and launched himself toward Alex.

Alex raised his own knife, his heart beating harder as he braced himself to fend off the infuriated king.

Then there was a hiss. A thunk. King Cassius gave a

grunt. He staggered one more step before his knife slipped from his fingers. He collapsed to the floor at Alex's feet.

For a moment, Alex just gaped down at the dead king—and the arrow sticking out of his back.

Then Alex dragged his gaze up, locking on where Daemyn stood several yards away, a bow in his hands. Colonel Beshko lay at his feet amid a pool of blood while Rosanna stood at Daemyn's back, holding his quiver. She'd smuggled Daemyn's weapons into the castle underneath the layers of her buckskin skirts.

"How many kings is that now?" Alex wasn't sure if it was the relief or the shock that made his voice come out somewhere between a sigh and a laugh.

"Hopefully that was the last one." Daemyn lowered his bow, his shoulders easing.

King Cassius had made his choice. He had decided he would rather go down fighting rather than go through a trial and execution. At least his actions had saved Alex the hassle of having to arrange all that.

Now Alex just had to send King Cassius's body back to Pohatomie and inform Queen Uma she was now a widow.

If the rumors were to be believed, she wouldn't be all that sad about the news.

On the dais, Kezzie stepped around her brother and picked up the crown. "Crown of the high king, I reckon you are eager to be back on the right head."

Alex took the crown from her, holding her gaze for a long moment before he placed the crown on his head.

It had been a long road to return here, but Alex was once again where he belonged. Though he hoped beyond hope that the mountain princess before him would realize she belonged here at his side.

Chapter 26

Keziah

Kezzie swung her legs back and forth as she perched on one of the cots in the castle's infirmary, ignoring the way the new stitches and bandage tugged as she moved.

She'd gotten a small slice to one of her legs as they hurtled through the window. Despite all their wounds gushing blood, her brothers had insisted that the physicians tend her first.

Now she was waiting as the physician and nurses tended her brothers. Most of them had cuts and scrapes from diving through the window. Zeph had a slice seeping blood across his cheek while Zeb had an injury to his arm. Josiah had a gash across his torso.

But it was Ezra who had the worst wound. Now that he was human again, his arrow wound was a puncture all the way through the muscle of his upper arm just above his elbow. All the strenuous flying had torn the injury open again, and blood coated his arm all the way down to his fingers. At least he hadn't suffered any additional wounds from the glass.

As the nurse was helping Ezra into a sling for his wounded arm, Alex strode into the room.

The nurse immediately dropped what she was doing to curtsy. The physicians and other nurses bowed or curtsied while all of Kezzie's brothers bowed.

Kezzie gripped the edge of the cot, too frozen to force herself to move. She hadn't had a chance to speak with Alex since her rescue.

Seeing him now, all the memories of traveling together flooded back, and her heart beat harder, a squeezing sensation in her chest. She both desperately wanted Alex to stop and speak with her and yet also didn't dare meet his gaze.

Alex glanced at her, but he halted by Josiah first, speaking with him in a low voice. Josiah laughed, and then Alex was moving on to Ezra, gesturing at his arm but still speaking too softly for Kezzie to hear what he said from where she sat.

Why did that squeezing feeling get even worse as Alex spoke with her brothers one by one? It seemed strangely right, seeing Alex among her brothers as if he belonged.

She'd never found herself envisioning anyone joining her family in that manner before, and it sent a little wiggly, flippy sensation through her stomach.

At last—or all too soon—Alex strode across the room until he was before her. He knelt before her, gazing up into her eyes. "Are you all right?"

She clenched her fingers tighter on the cot. How she longed to meet his gaze and actually *talk* to him.

Instead, she dropped her gaze, searching for something she could speak to.

Alex pressed a small carving into her hands. It was a

goose with its wings folded at its sides and its neck long and proud. "Now that your brothers aren't geese anymore, I thought you'd like to have something to talk to. I'd like to say I made this. Or even that I carefully picked it out and bought it myself. But, I'll admit, I sent into Eyota for it. I thought a small carved figurine that you could name would be easier to talk to instead of a random cot or moccasin or whatever."

Kezzie blinked. First at the carved goose in her hand, then at Alex. She swallowed several times, trying to find the words to speak. Alex's hands were warm around hers, sending tingles down her spine even as her chest tightened.

She cleared her throat, forced her fingers to tighten around the goose, and she held it up in front of her. "Should I name you after one of my brothers?"

"Not me." Josiah's voice came from just behind Alex a moment before he appeared over the high king's shoulder. "But he looks kind of like Ezra."

Ezra rolled his eyes, his arm now in a sling. "No thanks. I don't want my goose form to live on forever. But maybe Zeb wouldn't mind."

Zeb gave a noncommittal grunt.

Zeph grabbed both Josiah and Ezra by the backs of their collars. "Come along, everyone. Let's find Uncle Daemyn and see if he has any orders."

"But shouldn't we—" Ezra began.

Zeph gave him a harder tug. "No."

Josiah's eyes widened as he glanced between Kezzie and Alex. "Right. Yes. Let's go."

Zeph and Zeb hauled a still protesting Ezra between them as Josiah herded all of them before him.

When they had vacated the infirmary, the nurses and

physicians busied themselves at the far side of the room, as if trying to be invisible.

Alex turned back to her, a lopsided smile creasing his face. "Ezra will probably hate it, but the goose really does look like him as a goose."

"Yes, you do," Kezzie told the little carved goose. "Well, Little Ezra, the high king was asking how I was. I'm fine. Just a little cut on my leg."

"I'm glad you weren't hurt any worse. I heard that was quite the escape attempt, though I only saw the end of it."

"I was quite impressed with my brothers. You would have been too, Little Ezra." Kezzie ran a finger down the wooden goose's neck, as if petting it.

"If you're all right enough to walk, would you like a stroll along the battlements?" Alex held out a hand to her.

Still holding the goose in one hand, she rose to her feet, wishing she could take Alex's proffered hand. Instead, she rather vaguely flapped her hand at her side. Alex must have taken the hint since he snagged her hand, clasping it.

As they left the infirmary, she didn't let go of his hand, and he didn't let go of hers. It just felt right, strolling at his side hand-in-hand.

They made their way through several passageways and up a staircase until they exited onto the wall top where it overlooked the cliffs and the Kanawhee River far below. The lights of Eyota glittered in swirling reflections on the river.

Alex led them out into the center of the parapet, but he didn't let go of her hand to lean against the battlements.

Instead, he turned to her, squeezing her fingers. In the darkness, his eyes were liquid and deep as his gaze searched her face. "Kezzie, I don't know if you feel the same way I do. But while traveling with you, I saw your strength and resilience. I admire you, and I'm falling for you."

Kezzie's heart hurt with the hope of it. But also the pain. Because even as she held his gaze and the words piled onto her tongue, she couldn't speak them. And she wasn't about to speak these kinds of words to a wooden goose.

A tear trickled down her face as she held up the goose, her voice rough as she forced out the words. "The high king is very kind. But surely he knows that I could never be high queen. I can't even speak to people. What kind of queen could I be with my curse?"

Alex lifted their clasped hands, pressing a kiss to her knuckles. "You'd be a great high queen. Your curse has made you kind and compassionate. Because of your curse, you've learned to listen and to take the time to think before you speak."

He still didn't understand. To make him understand, she'd have to say the words to a wooden goose.

The wooden goose was blurring before her with tears. "Little Ezra, you see it, don't you? What kind of relationship could he have with me? With someone who can never speak her heart to his face. Who can never tell him she loves him. Who can never tell her children she loves them. What kind of life would that be?"

"Kezzie." Alex cradled her cheek with a hand, tipping her head so that she was looking at him. "Curses are made to be broken. But even if yours is never broken, we rest in the peace of the Highest King. Kezzie, I hear you, even if you can never speak to me directly."

He was looking at her with such trust in his eyes, begging her to trust in return.

That was the crux of her problem, wasn't it? She struggled to see beyond her curse. She didn't trust the Highest King's promises that her curse would be broken.

Back there in the forest when she'd been captured, the Highest Prince had told her to trust. Yet she was doing it again and not trusting him.

She had good relationships with her family, and up until recently, she'd never been able to speak to them. But it had never mattered. They were family, and they loved each other. If she could manage deep relationships with her family, then surely a romantic relationship wasn't as out of reach as she had thought.

For a moment, she squeezed her eyes shut and clung to the memory of that dream or whatever it was of the Highest Prince. If she dwelt with him, then her curse didn't matter. She might wrestle. She might doubt. But in the end, she had to cling to trust no matter the darkness. As the Highest Prince had said, no curse could stand between him and her. And if the curse was already broken there, then surely it wouldn't stand between her and Alex either. Not when it came to the heart.

When she opened her eyes again, Alex was still there, still cradling her face, still waiting for her answer.

How could she answer him? This seemed like the moment for sweet words or, better yet, a kiss.

But she couldn't even initiate a kiss because that was too much communication for her curse.

Maybe something of her longing showed in her eyes for Alex traced his thumb over her cheek. "May I kiss you?"

A question she could answer easily enough by talking to her little wooden goose. She dropped her gaze to it, fighting both tears and a smile. "Little Ezra, could you please tell the high king that he most certainly may kiss me?"

"Thank you, Little Ezra, for relaying the message." Alex clasped his hand over hers around the goose, lowering the hand between them. Then, he leaned forward and kissed her.

If her knees had been going weak before, she was downright wobbly now. But the castle wall was solid behind her, and Alex's hand was steady around her waist.

Perhaps it was the kiss, but starbursts were going off behind her eyelids. Her brain was just foggy enough that she murmured without thinking about it, "I wish I could tell you how much I'm falling for you too."

Alex froze, his hand tightening at her waist. "Kezzie?"

Her brain caught up, and her eyes flew open. She stared right up into Alex's gaze, very intentionally speaking to him. "I'm falling for you."

The words didn't stick in her throat. Her tongue didn't refuse to move.

She *spoke* to Alex.

"Your curse..." Alex trailed off, as if he couldn't bring himself to say it out loud.

"It broke. It really broke. Just like that." Kezzie's mind whirled, and she was thankful for Alex's steadying hand keeping her upright.

After all her fears, all her distrust, the Highest King had used this moment to break her curse. As she'd been reminded again and again, no curse could stand before him.

The curse must no longer serve his purposes. Now, his purpose was for her to speak. To be a voice for the voiceless as she reigned at Alex's side as high queen, never forgetting what it had been like to be denied her own voice for so long.

Alex grinned and tugged her closer. "I love it when the

Highest King uses me as a cursebreaker. But I am especially honored to be *your* cursebreaker."

Kezzie would revel in that later. But right now, she used her newfound freedom to stand on her toes and kiss him again.

Epilogue

One Year Later

Keziah

Kezzie swiped the lines of black paint over her face from the jar of grease paint Uncle Daemyn had brought to her sitting room in Castle Eyota where she, her brothers, Uncle Daemyn, Rosanna, and Alex were all gathered.

Kezzie glanced past the chaos of her brothers smearing on the grease paint to where Alex sat in a cushioned chair to one side, holding Uncle Daemyn and Rosanna's daughter Anna May. "You can come on the hunt too, Alex. You don't have to stay behind."

Alex lifted his gaze from the baby to raise his eyebrows at her. "It isn't traditional for the bride and groom to go on the hunt together."

"It ain't traditional for the bride to conduct the hunt either. It's usually done by the groom." Kezzie raised her eyebrows right back at him. Even a year later, she couldn't get over the freedom to banter right back.

She still had the wooden goose in her pocket. A reminder of the Highest King's faithfulness, even as she adjusted to life with her curse broken.

"Yes, well, of the two of us, you are the far more accomplished hunter. I bring a lot of things to this marriage—a crown, a castle, seven kingdoms to rule—but the ability to provide by hunting isn't one of them." Alex gave an exaggerated shudder. "Besides, I've gone on a buffalo hunt with the Rand Clan before. I ain't about to do that again."

Uncle Daemyn grinned at Alex, the look rather fierce with all the paint on his face. "I reckon not. You got a mite squeamish about all the blood."

"It wasn't the blood but the part where I was nearly trampled to death that made me squeamish." Alex gave another shudder, then waved with just his fingers to avoid jostling the baby in his arms. "Go off, be a Rand, and enjoy a wild romp through the mountains. I'm rather content to stay here and babysit."

If Kezzie's heart melted at the sight of Alex with a baby in his arms, well, it was a good thing she was marrying him the next day.

As nervous as she'd been about the prospect of becoming high queen, she'd found herself slowly falling in love with the role as she spent time at Alex's side. As the future high queen, she had the chance to talk to so many people from all over Tallahatchia, fellowshipping in a way she'd never had the chance to experience before.

Rosanna rolled her eyes as she settled into a seat across from Alex. "You're happy to babysit, until the diaper needs changing."

"Uncles don't change diapers." Alex grimaced, though the expression turned into a funny face as he said to Anna May, "Uncle Alex."

The baby might be only a few months old, but Alex was already hard at work to ensure that his name was one of her first words.

Josiah rolled his eyes, gripped Kezzie's shoulders, and steered her toward the door. "All right, that's enough lovey-dovey looks. Time for the hunt."

Kezzie shot Alex one last look over her shoulder before her brothers hustled her from the room, Uncle Daemyn at their heels.

As they strode down the corridors, the servants gave them a wide berth, side-eyeing their rather rugged buck-skins. But Kezzie wasn't about to hide who she was. She was a princess of the mountains, raised as one of the Rand Clan. Tallahatchia had better be prepared for who they were getting as their high queen.

As they exited the keep, Castle Eyota's courtyard bustled with her family, all of them carrying their weapons. To one side, Zeke passed his and Isi's daughter to Isi before he joined the crowd gathering for the hunt.

While not quite as many Rands had gathered for her wedding as they had Uncle Daemyn's, there were still a lot of them. All the Buckhannock Rands were here, both the castle Rands and the mountain Rands, led by Zeke and Asa.

But a few of the Tuckawassee Rands had come, including Aunt Frennie and her brood. Those wilder Rands weren't about to miss a good shindig.

Others would be there too, but in a more official capacity. The high king was getting married, and all Tallahatchia would be there to celebrate, Rand or not.

Josiah stuck his fingers in his mouth and gave a shrill whistle.

The gathered Rands quieted, turning toward them.

Zeph rested a hand on Kezzie's shoulder, smiling at her before he turned to the crowd. "All right, then. Let's get my sister hitched in proper mountain fashion!"

Kezzie's grin stretched so wide her cheeks hurt, even as her heart warmed in her chest.

After so many years of feeling lonely and cut off from her own family, this was proof that she had been loved all along.

DAEMYN

With the morning fog still thick over the river and wrapped around the mountains, Daemyn strolled Castle Eyota's wall top.

A figure leaned against the battlements, shrouded in the swirling fog.

Daemyn meandered toward him, leaning against the wall top next to him. "I thought I'd find you here."

Alex huffed a breath, swirling the fog around him. "We've come a long way since that day, haven't we?"

"Yes." Daemyn stared out at the misty mountains. "Never would have guessed back then that I'd be honored to have you marry one of my nieces."

Alex bowed his head for a moment, as if he didn't know how to respond to that. When he lifted his head, his tone was light. "After today, I'll officially be family. Does that mean I get to call you Uncle Daemyn?"

Daemyn stilled, not sure why those words created such a visceral reaction inside him.

Alex must have seen some of his horror on his face, for his smile, too, dropped, as did his shoulders. "I see."

"No, it ain't whatever you're reckoning." Daemyn half-turned to better face Alex. "I love that my family calls me Uncle Daemyn. But you're different. You're one of the few people left alive who knew me as Jadon. You're a friend—a brother—more than a nephew."

From the time they were ten—perhaps from the day they were born—Alex and Daemyn had been linked in a strange, destiny kind of way. They had come a long way from being an arrogant prince and invisible manservant. Soon they would be family by marriage, but they were already brothers from all they'd done and experienced.

Alex cleared his throat, taking a moment before he spoke in a voice rough with emotion, "All right then. Daemyn."

Daemyn let the silence linger between them for a minute before he laughed. "My brother Luke would be rolling in his grave if he knew you were marrying one of his great-great-granddaughters."

"Oh, he would have hated this." Alex, too, shook his head with a laugh. "I reckon he would have actually killed me back then if he'd known."

"Likely." Daemyn's brother Luke had not taken to the high king at all. Granted, Alex hadn't been at his best back then. But Luke wasn't the type to take to anyone not born on the mountains. Though, he must have changed his tune, as he eventually had a castleborn daughter-in-law.

Alex's grin took on a touch of a smirk as he eyed Daemyn. "Speaking of family, you do realize that as of today, your nieces and nephews now sit on the thrones of three of the kingdoms of Tallahatchia, including the throne of high queen, and you have family ties to a fourth kingdom. You've basically taken over Tallahatchia. I love Kezzie.

But it doesn't hurt politically that I married into the most influential family in all of Tallahatchia."

Daemyn shifted and grimaced. He'd really hoped no one would notice that.

The Buckhannock royalty were all Daemyn's relatives, descended from his brother Luke. Alex, the high king and ruler of Kanawhee, would soon marry Daemyn's great-something niece. Daemyn himself had married Rosanna, princess of Neskahana.

To everyone's surprise, Queen Uma of Pohatomie had married Stefan Vinzen, the castle seneschal and another one of Daemyn's nephews, only nine months after King Cassius's death. For both their sakes, Daemyn was glad that the match seemed to be one of love.

Queen Uma was the older sister of Queen Tamya of Tuckawassee, creating a tangential familial tie to that kingdom as well.

Only Monongadotte and Guyangahela didn't have a family tie in some way, though enough of his distant nieces and nephews were in influential positions in those king-doms to sway the politics there.

"I ain't done it on purpose." Daemyn ducked his head. Despite all the years he'd lived and the things he'd done, he was still just a poor boy from the mountains at heart. He'd never meant to steal power away from Alex's position as high king.

"That's what makes it so ironic." Alex clapped him on the shoulder. "You might have taken over Tallahatchia, but you're so loyal that it never occurred to you to use the power you currently wield in any way but to secure my throne. If Tallahatchia has peace, it's thanks to you and your family. I won't forget that."

Peace. Daemyn closed his eyes, savoring the word. Peace

to raise his daughter and any other children the Highest King might grant to him and Rosanna. Peace to see his nieces and nephews thriving. Peace to witness Alex rule as the high king he was always destined to be.

There was a time he'd thought he'd never experience it apart from the final peace found Beyond.

How richly he'd been blessed in the years since Alex had awoken. How much he would have missed if the Highest King had granted his wish to take him to Beyond back then.

"I ain't about to forget it neither." Daemyn clapped Alex's shoulder in return as, together, they watched the sun rise over the mountains.

ALEXANDER

Alex strode up the side aisle past the gathered guests to the front of the Great Hall of Castle Eyota, dressed in a silk shirt salvaged from his wardrobe from a hundred years ago, paired with white buckskin trousers. His mother walked at his side, her head held high even as she blinked away her tears.

Daemyn held the station at Alex's other side, standing as Alex's family, even if he should, by rights, walk with Kezzie and her family.

Alex's stepfather and stepsiblings had the first row, a place of honor, even if they weren't walking with Alex.

From here, Alex could barely see the cluster of people who were Kezzie and her family as they strolled up the aisle on the far side of the great hall.

Between them, rows upon rows of benches filled the

Great Hall. Between Kezzie's family, the Rand Clan, all the kings and queens of Tallahatchia, many of the nobles, and as many of the common folk who could fit, the room was filled to bursting.

At the end of the aisle, Alex climbed the steps to the dais.

There, King Omri of Buckhannock waited to officiate, standing a few feet in front of the thrones. Before him, resting on a stand below the center of the steps, lay the canoe Alex and Kezzie had built together and subsequently dubbed Falada II. It was filled with the hide of a buffalo that Kezzie and the Rands had hunted down the day before. Kezzie had also placed her bow and arrows in the canoe to signify what she brought to the marriage—the Rand toughness and legacy. On top of her bow and arrows, he had placed a crown. Funny how small a mere crown felt.

Across the way, Kezzie's parents and brothers climbed onto the dais, facing Alex. He couldn't see Kezzie as she was too obscured by her family.

King Omri glanced between them, then intoned the traditional words of the ceremony. "We are gathered here today to join in marriage Princess Keziah of Buckhannock and High King Alexander of Tallahatchia. Who brings this woman to this man?"

"We do." Kezzie's parents and brothers all spoke at once, even as they parted to finally reveal Kezzie standing behind them.

Alex's breath caught in his throat. She smiled almost shyly at him, her black hair loose and long around her shoulders, obscuring much of the beadwork on her white buckskin dress.

She was the most beautiful woman he'd ever seen. Not because of the fancy dress or the crown he'd soon place on her head. But because of her smile, her grit, her joy in speaking with the people of Tallahatchia. She was the woman he wanted to paddle down the river with all the days the Highest King would grant them.

"And who brings this man to this woman?"

"We do." This time, it was Alex's mother and Daemyn who spoke the words.

And then Alex was stepping forward and clasping Kezzie's hands. The ceremony passed in a blur of words Alex didn't hear. Then King Omri was pronouncing them man and wife, and Alex was kissing Kezzie, his blood rushing loud in his ears. Only the hoots and hollers of Kezzie's brothers were enough to pierce the noise.

Alex had waited a hundred years, survived four curses, and fought off more attempts on his life than he cared to remember to reach this happy ending.

And, Highest King willing, it would only be their beginning.

ACKNOWLEDGMENTS

Thank you so, so, so much to all of you readers who stuck through the long wait until this book finally released! I hope you enjoyed Alex's happy ending (finally!).

Thank you to my family for all your support over the years! Thank you to my friends, both writer and non-writer, for all your encouragement to finish this book! A special shout out to Bri for the idea for Kezzie's curse! Another shout out for Writer Group for helping me polish this mess of a book.

Thank you to Bethany, Deborah, and the ARC readers for finding the typos and inconsistencies!

But most of all, thank you to my Heavenly Father who is there even in doubts and struggles.